The Price
of Dust

A Tale from the Shadow's Path

By Auden S. Howard

While every precaution has been taken in the preparation of this book, the publisher assumes no responsibility for errors or omissions, or for damages resulting from the use of the information contained herein.

THE PRICE OF DUST

First edition. September 23, 2024.

Copyright © 2024 Auden S. Howard.

Written by Auden S. Howard

Prologue

Give me Liberty

26th of June, 2252

*"Stand amongst the ashes of a trillion dead souls,
and ask the ghosts if honour matters.
The silence is your answer."*

Governor Thayne Barrick stepped up to the podium, flanked on either side by Martian Defence Service guards. In the middle of the crowd stood a young Martian woman of auburn hair, dark eyes, and a worried smile. Celise knew there was something off about the guards, but she couldn't quite place it. She hadn't planned on spending her birthday at an address, but Syrin had begged her to come. Apparently, something big was going down. Celise shivered in the cold Martian air, silently wishing her parents had paid better attention to the colonial invitation ads. Sure, it was breathable these days, but hospitable was a stretch. She looked around the open square, noting the perimeter MDS guards; there seemed to be an awful lot of them. She kept scanning their faces, searching for the one she couldn't find. *Syr had better show up; I didn't come out here for nothing*, thought Celise. The Martian Governor was raising his hand for silence now. Whatever the big announcement, it was about to begin.

"From dust..."

Six Hours Earlier

"Cel! Wake up!" Celise groggily rubbed the sleep from her eyes. "Really, Syr? What time is it?" she mumbled through the lingering oh-so-sweet lull that had been suddenly shattered. Celise squinted her eyes open; a dim sliver of light shone in through their window from the planet's moons. She glanced at the readout on the wall next to the bed. 05:27. Far too early to be conscious. Then again, she couldn't fault Syrin. Her wife simply wanted to make the day as great as could be, and to her, that meant starting early.

"You know," Celise started, slowly waking more, "birthdays don't *have* to be so special *every* year." Syrin was Earth-born, and those people had some mighty strange traditions. Birthdays were one Celise adopted for her, not one she understood so much, though.

Syrin looked down at her wife, and Celise felt once again in danger of being lost in her eyes, eyes as green as the homeworld of their kind. "Oh, come on…" Syrin chided, all-too-chipper for the hour. "It's not just *any* birthday. It's your *champagne* birthday!"

Celise pushed herself into an upright position, groaning with the early-morning effort. She looked at her wife with confusion, "What in the moons does some outdated language have to do with my birthday? And would you keep it down? You'll wake up—"

Markil burst into his parents' room, carrying a platter of breakfast that Celise tried her best not to notice the scorch marks on.

"Happy birthday!" Syrin couldn't help but laugh. "Wake up, who now? And I don't know why it's called that, but it's when your age lines up with the day of the month, and it's extra special!" Celise forced her fatigued face muscles to respond to her brain's commands and smiled at little Markil. "Come here," she said, holding out her arms to wrap him in a big hug as he set down the platter.

"I made you breakfast in bed, Mum! We're out of coffee, though…" He offered her an apologetic smile. "Oh, don't worry about that. Thank you, sweetie, this looks amazing!"

Celise heard a small beep, and Syrin glanced at her wrist. Her face jumped from overwhelming joy to overwhelming disappointment in a half-second. Always quick on her feet, she recovered quickly enough that Markil didn't notice.

"Hun, why don't we leave your Mum to enjoy her breakfast, eh? We can open presents later." She turned to mouth an "I'm sorry" to Celise, along with a look that told her how important it was. Cel sighed, leaning back against the wall as the door closed.

"Alright, bud, no more stalling."

Markil gave Celise a look of mock innocence as he turned to finalize packing his bag. "You know I like my class; why would I be stalling?" he protested lightly.

His mother shook her head slightly, recalling her own attempts to delay having to go to school. Markil seemed to be doing okay here, but ever since their move to the capital, she couldn't stop worrying. Worrying even about the little things, like how quickly he could make friends. Her son slung the pack over his shoulder and gave her a quick hug goodbye.

"From dust," she called after him as he descended the steps from their little house. "To stone." Markil finished the traditional Martian call and response. He would never admit it, but secretly, he quite liked all the weird old-timey traditions she insisted on teaching him. As Celise stepped back inside, she checked her wrist for what felt like the hundredth time since the morning. Nothing, Syrin still hadn't checked in. *It's fine.* She told herself quietly. Twelve years, she had been with the woman who chased after danger—eight years since Syr had first joined the MDS. Even still, after all this time, it never got easier. Celise stepped over to the wall to call up her messages. She had a lot to read through from friends and family, far and wide, offering birthday messages. Some meant it; however, like her, most did it mainly for Syrin's sake, to help keep the tradition alive. Cel paused the scrolling, staring at a message she hadn't expected to see. *Joren*. If ever there was a man who detested technology, it was Joren. He *never* messaged; either he would tell you something in person, or from his perspective, it didn't need to be said. She felt the subtle pressure of anxiety building until—*No*. She would not allow herself to spiral, not today. Shutting down the wall, she moved to the door to gather her belongings and put on a light coat. She had to get out, just for a little while.

The Martian capital was abuzz with movement, with people, so many people. Celise still hadn't quite gotten used to just how many there were; back home in her little house overlooking Valles, there were maybe twenty families all-told making up a village. Here? Well, there had to be over 100,000 people. She pulled the frock tighter around herself, silently wishing she had grabbed the thicker jacket as the cold wind bit her exposed skin. A tall man bumped into her as she fussed with the clothing; he paused briefly to offer an apologetic smile.

"Peace through stars," he spoke to her. No, *sang* to her. She noticed with a start the man's deep blue eyes, that so *unnatural* colouring, coupled with his lilting words, he was *Venusian*. Cel had met a cloud-born only once before, and they had seemed an alright sort. Still, as she nodded a pardon to the man and continued moving, she could feel a growing sense of unease. What was that... The words! She realized with a start what he had said; it was the motto of the *Commonwealth*. Celise felt a slow, graining distaste forming. Two years prior, the Commonwealth of Sol was proclaimed from Null Station in the Gulf of Guinea on Earth. Lots of politicians singing out their big sweeping promises. She knew the truth. They were just trying to convince the people who had laid down their arms to keep them down.

The Fifth World War had committed massive devastation across Africa, Southern Europe, and the Middle East. When it was over, the nations of victory blamed it all on *autonomy*. They claimed that the Vanguard system, from before the war, which saw nations retaining some semblance of independence, was the cause of all their strife. Never mind, of course, the tens of thousands of Martian Expeditionaries whose lives had been cut short. Back then, Mars was under almost direct control of the Vanguard. And now, these bumbling fools had the *audacity* to claim that centralization was the only way to peace? No, Celise didn't have much hope for a future under *their* rule. She was proud to call herself Martian and proud of the Governor's efforts towards *more* autonomy.

She felt a drop land on her head and gazed up to red skies. Proud as she was, that didn't mean she had to love the weather's mood swings. Cel quickly hurried along, then ducked into a small café out of the sudden rainfall. The quiet little harmony was a welcome reprieve from the hustle and bustle outside. There weren't many folks here, just the one at the counter and a couple benching in the back. Celise walked up to order, grabbing her favourite delicious (but not entirely healthy) caffeinated duster. Finding a seat, she looked out the darkened windows to the world beyond. She always found it a bit of a strange feeling, the idea that a little pane of glass was all that separated her from the chaos beyond. She liked to imagine, sometimes, how it might feel to voyage through the stars and how similar it would be.

The quiet rambling from the screen at the back wall of the café grew louder as one of the patrons asked for it to be turned up. Cel turned to watch, smiling as her favourite person in the world filled the screen.

"We're taking all necessary precautions, I can assure you, and the rest of Mars, that their governor is, as always, in good hands," Syrin spoke with a warm yet formal tone in addressing the reporter. Her green-blue-white suit was a proud mirror to the Martian tricolour. Of course, it was still stained by the flag of the Commonwealth on each shoulder, but some things just couldn't be helped. The screen snapped to switch viewpoints, displaying the reporter. He was an older man and spoke with a pronounced Martian accent. Celise's smile grew; Andai Kirstnia was the anchor on her favourite show; he always knew just what questions to ask and still kept things light.

"What can you tell our listeners about the address itself, Marshal? Anything we should be waiting for?" Celise felt her wrist buzz with a new message. "Well"—the cam snapped back to Syrin—"I know that Governor Barrick will want to save most of it as a surprise. However, what I can tell your listeners is that it absolutely pertains to them. Governor Barrick wants to lead the Martian people as best he can, and his speech this afternoon will be groundbreaking in that endeavour." Syrin turned slightly, facing someone off-cam. "I'm sorry, Mr. Kirstnia, but that looks like all the time I have for you. I hope to see you there."

Markil jumped high in the Martian gravity to catch the disc flying tall and fast past him in the playground. He missed it, only just, and his new friends let out a collective laugh. Markil picked himself back up off the dusty surface.

"Next time!" his friend called. Despite the rampant tension elsewhere, he felt a growing sense of belonging here. Markil used to play discs back in the old town, of course, and everyone else did, but the city folk had another version. It seemed somehow more... competitive. Markil wasn't sure he liked it so much. The game continued, mostly in his team's favour, for the duration of their break.

When the bell finally rang, he was entirely out of breath, much more than he thought he should have been, for all the contribution he had made to the game. Markil looked up to the starry sky beyond as he gathered his belongings. It was a clear day, and he could make out the tiny pinpricks of light that were a testament to the vastness of the wider universe. He frowned slightly as something else caught his eye; it almost looked like a ship? If it was, it was flying entirely too low and moving far too fast. The object was highly reflective, whatever it was, and Markil could make out the faint shape of some sort of text alongside it. He squinted up, trying to force his eyes to decipher the blurry message.

Celise sat still in the café, staring blankly at the text from Joren. She knew she shouldn't have read it.

Elly, I hear it's your birthday, so I'm sorry to be the bearer of bad news today, of all days. This can't wait; something is coming here; all the MDS personnel were called away this morning. When they returned, something was definitely wrong. Some of them were missing, and those that had returned didn't offer the smiles we've come to expect, only cold stares. Something's up with the uniforms as well, I can't say what for sure. Word is that Governor Barrick will be addressing the colony this afternoon. El, listen to me, you must *be there.*

One last thing. No matter what, don't trust Syrin.
~ Joren

Celise's heart was beating faster than she ever thought possible. Its rapid movement was at odds with her own statue-like state. Syrin? What in the moons could Joren have found? How could he ever think Syrin was hiding anything? No. Cel wouldn't keep dwelling on this. She shook herself back to reality and gathered her things. Stepping out of the small shop, she looked up to see the rain had stopped. Martian weather was certainly as flippant as ever. Her wrist buzzed, and glancing down, she felt a swell of relief. It was Syrin.

Hey, love, sorry about this morning. Something came up. Please be at the square.

Celise tried not to frown at the non-helpful explanation. She sent a quick reply, *See you soon.*

Governor Barrick was pacing back and forth in front of his office window.

"You're absolutely certain?" he pushed, stopping to stare intensely at Syrin. "Yes, sir. The reports are conclusive. The Commonwealth is en route." She stood at attention before his office door, highly aware of the discrepancies between her own and the other guards' uniforms. She didn't like those discrepancies.

"Very well, give the order, Marshal. We will begin at once."

The square was already packed when Celise arrived. Her eyes started scanning the outskirts, where the MDS guards were, for any sign of Syrin. Typically, she would have been very visible and close to the governor. For whatever reason, though, that wasn't the case today. Governor Barrick stepped closer to the podium and raised his hands to quiet the large crowd. Cel couldn't stop glancing at the guards; something was definitely wrong.

As the assembled citizens became silent, the Governor began his speech. "From dust..." he started, and the crowd erupted with the traditional Martian response. "To stone!"

"People of Mars, we have long toiled under the rule of the Earth. Our farms have been made to feed *them*; our goods have been sent to please *them*. I ask you, what have you seen in return?"

The cries of the crowd were decisive and unified. Celise felt herself getting drawn into the whole spectacle.

"For how long must our children *die*? Die in *their* wars?" The Governor was positively preaching now, and Celise, a proud Martian, felt a gnawing sense of unease grow within her.

"I say this to you now, fellow Martians. No more! We have asked, then begged, and now pleaded for the Commonwealth government to hear our concerns. Not once have they responded!" Celise looked around the circle, searching for Syrin, to no avail. Then it hit her; the uniforms! The Commonwealth flag was missing from the MDS uniforms!

"In accordance with the Commonwealth's own founding charter, on behalf of the people of Mars, I hereby invoke The Stellar Mandate! Section 2.2.5 of the Codex Cosmica, our duty to rebel!" The cheers of the crowd had grown even louder now, and Celise realized that she had, in fact, joined in.

"Henceforth, the Republic of Mars shall be free and independent!" The cheers erupted into a roar of passion, of concurrence, of unity. As the noise from the square continued at a steady rate, Celise heard another, higher-pitched sound rising. She thought it was her mind playing tricks at first until she looked up, and everything went black.

1

Give me Death

26th of June, 2252

"Sacrifice is a choice you make.
Loss is a choice made for you."

The sky was covered by a thick cloud of inky smoke as Celise slowly pried open her eyes and immediately wished she hadn't. The soot burned her exposed vision. People were running, falling, she imagined screaming, though she couldn't hear it. The ringing sound in her ears was all-consuming, unrelenting in its incessant assault on her senses. She slowly forced her muscles to respond, to move, to try to rise, only to find she was pinned under a fallen statue. Celise lay back, staring up at the chaos unfolding all around her. She watched as the sleek, shiny darts tumbled down from the sky and massive plumes of flame and debris shot up from their impact. She was suddenly aware of a hand gripping her shoulder, and she twisted as much as the debris would allow, seeing the terrified eyes of her wife looking down at her. Syrin's mouth was moving, but even as Celise began to hear the world around her once more, the words were lost to a hellish din. Syrin could see her voice being lost and began to pull and pry at the statue. With an effort, Celise was free, free to be crushed beneath the weight of a thousand questions. Each one clambering for urgent attention. Chief among them came rushing to her mind: Markil. Celise realized her mouth had moved then, and Syrin's face suddenly flashed to a mirror of her own worry. Words needed no wasting as the pair moved quickly and carefully through the ruins of the once powerful centre. Bodies littered the square, what should have been a place of joy, of victorious wonder. Celise felt her eyes being drawn to each one in turn. She felt her head swim at the twisting sight of horror all around her. Syrin grasped her arm, eyes straight ahead. She supported Celise as they picked their way out of the immediate aftermath; it wasn't until they had turned onto the main street that they saw the rest. Stretching out into the distance lay a city in flames. Craters, toppled buildings, and debris were strewn everywhere.

They had been walking for around two hours, navigating through a mess of hazy warfare, when Syrin finally spoke again.

"I'm sorry I didn't tell you."

Celise kept moving; she only half heard her wife's words, and when she did hear them, she didn't pay them much mind.

"Cel, it was top secret; nobody was supposed to know." Celise laughed out loud briefly before the expression caught in her throat. She stopped walking, turning to face Syr. Syrin's face was drawn, tired, and had a mask of shock covering it.

"*Somebody* clearly knew," Celise said, almost dryly. Syrin stared into her eyes for a long few seconds, then shook her head slightly. "No. It's not possible."

Celise turned away, kept walking as a dry, humourless laugh escaped her lips. Syrin hurried to catch up.

"We'll be there soon; tell me about your day?" Celise shot her wife a sharp look, then paused momentarily to close her eyes. When she opened them again, her face had softened. Syrin asked that very thing of her every single day, every day when the work was done, when they saw each other once more; Syr began with that phrase.

"I heard from Joren," she said slowly, the unpleasant feeling of doubt seeping to the forefront of her thoughts.

"Oh? And what did our favourite professor have to say?" Syrin's tone was light, conversational. Cel knew what she was doing, and she was thankful for it.

"Just some ramblings, the usual conspiracy afoot. Except I guess this time he was right."

Now, it was Syrin's turn to send her wife a questioning look.

"What do you mean? He knew about the announcement?" Her voice carried a feeling of urgency, lightly masked.

"I'm not sure how much he knew," Celise started, "his message just told me I simply had to be there, that it was important. He basically sounded like you."

They rounded a corner onto the last stretch of road to Markil's school. Celise quietly wondered why she hadn't told Syrin the last piece of Joren's message; she didn't believe it, of course. She couldn't.

"When did you see him?" Syrin said, urgency returning to her voice. Cel's eyes offered her reassurance. "No, don't worry, Syr, he sent a message. I didn't see him in person."

Syrin's face was hardened in concentration, in deep thought. The pair continued walking steadily down the long, traumatized street, each step bringing them closer to a terrifying beacon of smoke in the distance. They moved with a whirlwind of emotion, threatening to topple them at any moment.

"That's not like Joren," Syrin finally said, "to send a message."

Celise pushed on. "No, it's not. That's what you're thinking about?"

Syrin went quiet again for a long time. Long enough that the school was well and truly near now. It was quiet and seemed to still be largely intact. The still form of the structure seemed contrary to the chaotic fervour enveloping the rest of their world. As they neared the entrance, Syrin offered Celise's hand a simple squeeze, the gesture small, carrying a shared anxiety. Outside the building, the ordinarily vibrant playground was deserted, and pieces of debris littered the ground. As did the bodies. Celise moved a few steps toward them before her wife caught her by the shoulder.

"No, look again."

Celise stopped and looked more carefully. There were… few. All of them were wearing uniforms of the Defence Service. She let out a silent breath in relief, wondering what horror that anointed to her.

Syrin and Celise entered the school and heard their footsteps echoing throughout the empty halls. Across the walls were colourful, joyous murals. Stories of history, art, and culture. Celise could have sworn they were mocking her. Each room they passed darkened her hope, the upturned desks and strewn supplies signalling an all-too-hurried evacuation.

"I just, I can't believe this is real," Celise murmured, her heart pounding with desperation. "That this is all really… *happening*." Syrin held her arm closer. "I know, love. But we must keep moving. Keep moving for him."

Finally, after what had felt like hours, the anxious parents reached Markil's classroom. Celise stepped across the threshold, feeling a wave of anticipation wash over her, feeling her breath catch in her throat. Syrin held firm at her side. Within, the room was empty, as devoid of the living as all the rest. Syrin's practised gaze swept the room and saw quickly the dull glow of the instructor's desk. She moved quickly to find the solemn note, her eyes scanning over the display and her brain picking out the critical pieces. Hurt. Shelter. Alive.

Syrin brushed a lock of hair out of her wife's eyes.

	"He's okay, love. He's alive. He... he will be."
Celise thought the flickering lights above were laughing at them until a low rumble shook the building, and the flickers stopped, plunging the staircase into darkness. Syrin took a final step to the bottom, her hand guiding the way through the void to their destination. The shelter was the farthest level of the school's basement. It had been designed years ago, before the terraforming was complete, to withstand the worst of Martian storms. Now, it offered protection from a manufactured disaster.

	As they grew closer to the entrance, the sounds of the outside world dimmed in their ears, replaced by the steady echoes of their footsteps. Syrin and Celise turned the final corner to find a small collection of people clustered in the dim light. Inside, children were gathered in the cramped space. Some of them appeared unaffected by the events, playing with whatever they could. Others were experiencing an all-too-obvious shell shock, huddling in the arms of the instructors. The air was thick here. It held a musty smell of damp concrete and the faint odour of medicine. Celise and Syrin's eyes swept over the assembly, searching with agony for the one face they needed, for Markil. Celise felt Syrin let go of her hand and saw as she stepped to one side of the interior, approaching one of the less-occupied adults. They spoke with urgency, in hushed tones Celise could not hear. In the dim light, she could not make out the instructor's expression. When Syrin turned, she didn't have to.

Before a word was spoken, Celise read the truth on her wife's face. Her legs failed, and Syrin caught her just before she reached the ground. The instructor was speaking gently; her voice was a soft murmur in the tense shelter's air. Their words faded away, becoming a distant hum as Celise felt her world narrowing into a spinning tunnel of grief. The light hum of the shelter's machinery, the cries of the children, and the comforting speech of the instructors dissolved into a void, until only the thunder of her silent scream remained. Her face, a mask of shock and terror, didn't make a sound. Syrin wrapped her arms around Celise, her own tears meeting with her wife's as they sank to the cold, uncaring stone, unified in a silent despair.

***

It was days later when Syrin finally heard the faint click of the door. After the shelter, Celise had fallen unconscious, and through her own pain, Syrin had carried her back up to the surface. It was there she awoke and, with urgency, ran to Markil's former classroom. The door was closed behind her, and she sank to the floor against the transparent barrier. Syrin had begged and pleaded for her to emerge, until she gave up the effort. Now, that door was sliding open with a hiss, Celise standing tall and silent as it did.

"Cel?" Syrin murmured, the word struggling to emerge from her dry throat. Celise opened her mouth as though about to say something, then, looking confused, closed it again. She stepped out of the old classroom, right past her wife, and began walking down the corridor to the exit. Syrin quickly hurried to catch up with Celise, who was moving at a brisk pace.

"Where are you going? What are we doing?"

Syrin's words may as well have not been said for all the response they garnered. Celise kept moving, pausing only briefly to push open the outer doors. She stepped out to the battered Martian streets, each stride long and purposeful. Syrin trailed behind, keeping pace, a litany of questions pouring out, none reaching Celise's ear. Her mind was in turmoil. A raging burn of anguish, determination, and a singular thought led her movements: vengeance. The journey through the city devastated by the Commonwealth's attack was a blur. The craters, fallen buildings, and littered wreckage were nothing but a backdrop to her innermost thoughts. Unbidden, remembrances of Markil flashed through her mind—laughter, curiosity, dreams. All of it cut off before it could ever truly blossom.

Finally, Celise reached her destination. Syrin came to a stop behind her, gazing up at the structure that had demanded her wife's presence so absolutely. It was a recruitment office of the Martian Defence Service. The building was staggeringly intact amongst all the destruction. Syrin moved forward quickly, keying open the outer door as Celise strode forth. The walls were adorned with flags and posters; they proclaimed the virtue of service to one's people. Behind the main counter stood a woman marking down notes on a display. Her gaze flicked up as Celise approached. The clerk opened her mouth for an instant, closing it again as Celise's sharp gaze reached her. The clerk nodded with a simple understanding and gestured to a door on one side of the room. Syrin caught her wife's hand in her own, and gave a gentle squeeze before letting go and stepping into the waiting area.

After what felt like a hundred questions and tests, Celise was stood before a short man wearing an officer's uniform. The man spent a few minutes examining the card in his hand before activating a recording device on one end of the chamber and stepping to one side.

"Please read from the display," he said simply, and the other end of the room flashed to life with a collection of text for her.

"I, Celise Valen, do solemnly swear to serve the Martian Defence Service, to uphold the principles of justice and freedom, and to dedicate my strength and spirit to the defence of the Republic of Mars, and to the protection of its citizens wherever they may be, in peace and war, as long as I shall serve, from dust to stone."

2

Price of Allegiance

14th of July, 2252
Eighteen Days Later

"It is possible to commit no mistakes and still lose. That is not a weakness; that is life."

The biting chill of Martian wind whipped across the tarmac, slashing at her face. The freeze it brought was a blunt contradiction to the heated emotions on the military base. Celise knew Syrin wouldn't be able to stay forever, but she had only been training for two weeks and didn't feel ready yet. They stood apart from the maddened movements of the base, their hands clasped tightly together as though they sought to pour every bit of feeling into what could be their final touch. The surrounding air was heavy, and the scent of fuel mingled with an aura of anxiety in the recruits. It was a most tangible reminder of the rapidly escalating war.

Syrin's uniform was pristine, as usual, and the signet of her rank reflected brightly in the early morning light. She looked every bit the officer she was, poised and determined, yet her eyes betrayed a deep well of emotion as she gazed upon Celise.

"I wish…" Syrin began, the words catching, desperately pleading not to be said. "I wish I didn't have to go." Her voice was barely audible and threatened to be drowned out by the roar of the engines and the thunder of marching boots. Her hands moved to adjust the strap of her helmet. It was perfectly adjusted already, of course.

Celise struggled to maintain a sense of composure and took Syrin's hand in her own again, squeezing tightly.

"I know, but you must lead them. You're not just going to fight, Syr, you have to set the example for all of us." Celise's voice cracked as she spoke, the sheer weight of her reality looming over her. Despite her recent enlistment, this new fear for her wife was overshadowing her burgeoning sense of duty.

Syrin nodded, understanding dancing through her eyes. She pulled Celise close into a tight embrace.

"I'll be careful, I promise. Just... take care of yourself too. The training here is tough, I don't want you getting hurt." Her words, muffled as they were against Celise's shoulder, carried a weight of equal comfort and ache.

Finally, as they parted, Syrin's eyes lingered on Celise as if she were trying to etch every detail of her face into memory.

"Remember your purpose," she urged; her tone was a mixture of plea and command. Celise nodded, her tears brimming but not yet spilling over. "For Markil." she breathed. His name, a sacred vow between them. She watched as Syrin turned away, her figure assuming resolve and authority as she marched toward the waiting officer's shuttle. Through all the turmoil, all the darkness, Celise felt a surging pride that the woman she loved remained a pillar of strength and resolve. The shuttle's engines flared with a deafening roar, casting a brilliant light across the pad. Celise shielded her eyes against the brightness, watching as the craft lifted into the sky, carrying Syrin to the front.

The recruit's barracks offered little in the way of comfort to Celise. Its pragmatic, utilitarian blandness was something she still hadn't gotten used to. The rows upon rows of bunks didn't give her much to look forward to. Supposedly, this was an intentional command decision. The MDS had originally been simply an enforcement branch of the Martian Judiciary and now was undergoing a rapid retrofit into a military service for their newly declared Republic. To that end, equipment was scarce, and once on deployment, Celise would have to get used to sleeping without any bunk at all. The ground wasn't so bad, she knew. She'd first met Syrin while lying back to gaze up at the stars one night... so long ago now.

A loud clattering brought her back to the present. Ensign Shay stood over a pile of equipment on the floor, his arms at his side and his face drawn with exasperation.

"Let me get that for you, Darek," Ensign Sorensen said, moving quickly to his side and dropping to one knee. Celise shook her head in mild amusement. Darek Shay was simultaneously the best shot of the trio and the most clumsy man she'd ever met. Of the six Ensigns that made up her squad, she'd only actually *met* these two. Supposedly, the Captain in charge of training here wanted them to be able to operate well in smaller groups first. Celise walked over to the pair, crouching to help Ata lift a particularly large desktop.

"What are you doing with this thing, anyway?" she asked the sharpshooter. "Don't you have a desk on your bunk?"

Darek gave her a sly grin. "That one tracks your calls, remember? *This* one, on the other hand..." He trailed off, dropping what he had collected and snapping quickly to attention. Ata and Celise got the hint, setting down the desktop quickly. They both turned and matched Shay's attention stance. Captain Vayan was standing in the doorway, expectantly.

"Your barracks is a mess. It *will* be clean the next time I step foot here. Report to the range in 30, dismissed." The officer marched away at a brisk pace, and the door hissed shut behind him.

Celise hadn't been to this part of the base before. As it turned out, the "range" Captain Vayan had referred to was not their standard firing line. Instead, it was a large building with the look of a warehouse to it. From where they stood behind a bright red line, Celise could see a large facility that resembled a house or shop, perhaps from the Capital. Only, there was no glass in the windows, no decorations on the walls. Everywhere, everything was coated in that same metallic sheen that had taken over her vision recently. Her fellow recruits turned with her at the sound of approaching footsteps. Three soldiers wearing Ensign uniforms like their own, and wearing the same diamond signets as them, stepped into the strange room. Suddenly, a wall panel snapped to life, its screen displaying the face of Captain Vayan, bringing all six recruits to attention.

"Welcome, recruits, to the Academy. This facility is designed to mimic real-world close-quarters combat environments. You'll have to excuse the patch-job state of it. The Academy was put together over the past few weeks from whatever we could find." The assembled squad exchanged slightly nervous glances with each other and the facility.

"You will move through this course in pairs. At randomized positions throughout, the Academy will display one of three types of target. If the target is equipped with a diamond pattern, like that of your signets, the target represents a civilian. If the pattern is a circle, the target represents a hostile. If the pattern is a single vertical bar, then hitting the target will result in an immediate failure for *all* of you."

With that, the screen winked out, and a crate on one end of the room popped open, displaying six identical rifles, painted in the colours of the Republic. Inside the crate, a simple display read, "Step across the red line to begin."

The assembled recruits relaxed their postures and turned to one another to introduce themselves. From the three newcomers, there was Lyan Jure, Talia MeGal, and Rai Borlo. Lyan and Talia quickly paired themselves up, each grabbing a rifle and moving toward the start line. Overhead, a hidden bulb somewhere flashed to green, bathing the prospects in a warm glow as a buzzer sounded. Talia and Lyan moved together, quickly and cautiously. Celise sat on the bench in the viewing area, turning her attention to a wall panel showing both recruits' cameras. Jure was from Earth, something that was pretty obvious in his movements. He must have arrived recently, as he still wasn't accustomed to the gravity of Mars. Celise felt an odd sensation in the back of her mind, like she was forgetting something, something she couldn't quite place. Almost with an absent mind, she swiped at her wrist, pulling up her messages. Pulsing there, with the notification that she hadn't replied to it yet, was Joren's.

Celise drew in a quick, quiet breath, her mind flooding and realization washing over her. *Don't trust Syrin,* he had said. Maybe what he really meant was... don't trust *Earth.*

The overhead buzzer blared, shaking her from her thoughts. The tally on the wall showed a score from Talia and Lyan, 78% accuracy, 89% judgment, and no total fails. Rai and Ata had stepped up to the starting line, waiting for the buzzer to permit them entry. That would leave Celise to complete her course with Darek; at least their accuracy score should be solid. As the light flashed again, Ata and Rai began to run the Academy, and Celise fell back into her thoughts.

If Joren's warning had been about the Commonwealth's attack... maybe he just didn't trust Syrin because she was from Earth? Celise shook her head. It didn't make any real sense, Syrin came here years and years ago... still, she wondered. There weren't very many details in her fellow cadets' personnel files, but she had learned *some* things. Things like why they were here, mostly. Talia was from a village not so far from Celise's own old home, a village that had been attacked in synchronization with the bombing at the capital. Rai didn't give much of a reason, but she knew he was a student before this. Ata was from the capital; she was a medic before the attack and joined up now to save lives closer to the action. Darek was here on the orders of a Martian court, though she didn't ask more. Finally, there was Lyan, the one from Earth. Who as far as his personnel file was concerned, hadn't actually *joined* the MDS as much as he had been drafted into it. Officially, there was no compulsory service here, not yet anyway, but Celise had to wonder if things might be a little different for an Earth-born.

The light and panel flashed once more, signalling the end of Ata and Rai's run. 77% accuracy, 91% judgment, and still no fails. Celise picked up a rifle and moved to meet Darek at the starting line. She knew it was only an exercise, that there was no enemy, nobody shooting back, but still, she could feel her heart beginning to pound in her chest. She gripped the rifle tighter, exchanging a cursory nod with Darek. Then the buzzer sounded, and the light flashed green. Celise moved slowly, too slowly, she knew, forward into the

Academy. Rounding the first corner, two targets dropped down from the ceiling; Darek quickly snapped up and squeezed the trigger, hitting the first enemy precisely in the centre. Celise was slower but still managed to take down her own target with a modicum of precision. The pair continued moving through the labyrinth-like facility, stopping only to sight their targets before continuing on. The further in they went, the better Celise started to feel. The adrenaline, maybe? She wasn't sure, but as they kept sweeping through, she had a feeling they were going to score quite well.

Celise found herself moving with newfound confidence through the metallic corridors, feeling the vibrating hum of the floor. Every step was lighter, and her aim steadier. They were doing well indeed, and a sense of accomplishment was washing over her. Suddenly, a target burst up from a vent in the floor directly between them, practically underfoot.

"Darek, look out!" Celise yelled as she stumbled back in surprise. Darek whirled around, his rifle already raised. He squeezed the trigger without fully acquiring his target, without taking the time to verify. The shot loudly echoed in the enclosed section, a sharp *crack* that made Celise flinch. Then she was aware of a jolt of pain lacing through her left arm like a wildfire and a metallic tang to the air. Her vision started to swim as she looked down at the arm, where a small red bloom was blossoming on the sleeve of her uniform.

Funny, Celise thought. She didn't remember passing out. Yet here she was, lying in a medical bay somewhere, and she certainly couldn't think of another explanation. With the force of a storm, her memory recovered as she looked down to see her left arm wrapped in bandages and propped up with a sling. The door at one end of the room slid open, and Captain Vayan stepped inside. His eyes looked over her, his gaze assessing but not unkind.

"Ensign Valen," he began, his voice carrying both the weight of his authority and the softening of concern. "You've had your first real lesson today. Combat is unpredictable, as is life."

Celise did her best to push herself into a more upright position but stopped as the pain in her arm shot through whatever medication she had been given.

"Yes, sir." she managed, "it won't happen again." Vayan chuckled softly, catching her by surprise. "Don't do that, Ensign. Don't make a promise on something beyond your control. Learn from this, yes, adapt from it yes, but do not place blame anywhere it doesn't belong." His eyes seemed to darken with that as he pulled a chair up next to her bed and took a seat.

"Tell me, Valen, why are you here?" His voice was softer, almost quiet in the small room, his eyes holding a quiet kindness within. "You must have read my personnel file, sir," Celise spoke out, her voice slowly returning.

Captain Vayan smiled slightly. "You're here because you believe in something, Ensign. Because you care about your home, about justice. That's honourable." Celise felt a small swell of pride from his words. "But remember, such ideals will only guide you. To stay alive, you will require more... practicality." The Captain shifted in his seat, looking around at the sterile walls surrounding them. "War," he continued, "is not about some singular moment of heroism, nor bravery. War is about endurance, Ensign, survival, and the achievement of your given objectives. Sometimes, that means making a difficult decision."

Captain Vayan stood, pushing the chair back into its resting position, and with a respectful nod, exited the chamber. Celise stared at the ceiling, the stark tiles blurring her vision into a foggy state as her thoughts drifted to Markil. His face was everywhere, strongest when she closed her eyes. The smile that once lit up their home had faded into memory, shrouded by the clouds of war. The pain in her arm seemed somehow far away, yet an ever-present calling to the life she would now live. She turned her head slowly to gaze out the small window at the side of her bed. Her home stretched out before her eyes, the tapestry of red and orange hues seemed to go on forever under a beautifully coloured sky. With a deep, steadying breath, Celise closed her eyes.

3

Baptism by Fire

13th of August, 2252
Thirty Days Later

"War never changes."

Celise jumped into the rapidly dug, shallow pit as enemy rounds slashed through the air all around her. She landed roughly on her still-healing arm and cried out sharply at the pain. Darek stood from the cover, firing off a few rounds back in the direction of the enemy before ducking down again.

"Cel! Your rifle!" Ata was shouting at her and pointing at the weapon lying on the lip of the foxhole. In her haste to take cover, she seemed to have dropped it. Celise bit back a curse as she rolled upright, quickly snatching the weapon from the pit's edge. The awful din of war was overwhelming her senses. The hazy smoke was everywhere. A crude scent that mixed the excesses from fire and Martian dust caught in the wind. Her ears were ringing. Both from the constant explosions and the screams of her comrades. And her eyes, to keep them open was her greatest challenge. The soot had them watering, and she was hard-pressed to look anywhere there wasn't a body laying.

"What are you all sitting around for! Get up here and flank that bunker!" Captain Vayan's sharp commands came out as a resonant bark, rising above the cacophony of pain surrounding them. "Yes, sir!" They cried in unison, pulling themselves to their feet and climbing out of the foxhole. One of their artillery pieces must have done its job, as a massive blanket of smoke was billowing from the enemy's primary position, blinding the foe to all movements.

The eager squad of soldiers rushed quickly to the side of the bunker, using the billowing cloud as a cloak. Darek and Ata readied themselves against one side of the looming entryway. Talia came up alongside Celise on their opposite, taking the breacher's position.

With a nod of commencement, the team moved steadily into the fortification. The air was heavier inside, thick with the scent of smoke and the flavour of war. A narrow corridor greeted their party, with small, occasional openings they took the time to clear with caution. Celise flinched as a gunshot rang out, and Ata lowered her weapon, having dispatched an enemy from one such aperture. The team kept their pace, senses heightened for signs of more hostility, but none came.

At last, they reached the end of the hallway. Here, the bunker opened into a small room with displays and charts adorning every available space. Darek signalled with his hand to a body slumped against a console of some kind, and the team fanned out to encircle their target.

As Celise lowered her rifle, her hand drifted absently toward her earpiece to summon Captain Vayan. Mid-reach, the movement was arrested by a stark puff of red, blooming from the centre-chest of the lifeless figure. Her reality—briefly—fractured. Time dilated around her as she processed the silent echo of a gunshot left in her mind. Celise turned slowly, almost dreamlike, to Talia, whose rifle was smouldering with a wisp of smoke curling upward. The strange moment hung in her mind's eye, an event frozen in time.

"Cel? Hello? You still in there?" Darek was... shaking her? Celise snapped back to reality, blinking away the ghosts of gunfire. The dusty, smoke-laden battlefield reasserted its presence upon her. Was she not inside a bunker? The drops of memory flittered away from her grasp as she mentally re-composed.

"Yes," she managed to speak out, the word sounding hollow and foreign to her ears. "Sorry, what were you saying?"

Darek's eyes softened slightly, "No worries, but you better listen up. Captain's debriefing soon." Celise looked around again, willing her eyes to see this time what had eluded her before. There was a large group of MDS personnel, all gathering around a small raised rock formation. Surrounding them was... war. Everything, everywhere, was twisted. So contorted that she could not make out the artificial from the formerly living. Vayan was standing atop the raised position, holding some kind of amplifier.

"Attention!" he called out to the assembly of delirium. Waiting a moment to allow their consideration to arrive his way, he began.

"You all fought well today, with the resilience and skill that are the hallmarks of our service. However, this is just the beginning." The Captain's eyes surveyed his soldiers, "We have new orders from High Command. In 24 hours, we will be deploying to Sector Seven of Coprates Chasma. Intelligence suggests a large force of Commonwealth Loyalists are amassing there for a major assault on the neighbouring villages. Your orders are simple: stop those attacks at all costs. For Mars!" The Captain stepped down from his make-do pedestal, the act of dismissal allowing the assembled soldiers to disband to various places. Many would be visiting the temporary medical tents for their wounds or the armoury for their gear. Not enough, Celise suspected, would be making for their beds. She didn't intend to make that mistake.

Twenty-Five Hours Later

"I thought there was supposed to be a massive force here..." Rai mumbled as their five-man team looped around the end of Sector Seven for the second time. Celise actually didn't mind the action-less patrol; it allowed plenty of time to think. She let her mind drift, to enter a wandering state of song echoed by past absences. As she walked, Celise felt her mind pulling her back to Markil.

It was particularly cold out that night in the park. Markil was shivering in the bitter winds that rolled along Valles. It was unclear for whose benefit he was pretending not to feel the sting. Syrin stopped walking so suddenly that Celise nearly stumbled over. "Something wrong?" she had asked. Syrin glanced quickly at Markil before forcing a smile and shaking her head slightly. Celise looked past her wife's soothing face. Just at the end of the visible path, maybe 30 metres or so along, there was a group of people huddling under a lamp. Celise squinted into the darkness, willing her eyes to see more until she did. There was a billowing piece of fabric being hung from the post. She didn't recognize the flag but could tell at least it was from one Earth nation or another. Syrin was pulling on Markil's arm now, trying to angle their family away along a different path. Celise followed along, seeing the strange look in her wife's gaze. It was an almost melancholic expression and resolved to find out more once Markil's young ears were further away. She was about to reach out to take Syrin's hand when the thunderous retort of a rifle exploded in her ears. Celise felt the frown spread across her face; this wasn't right. With a shock, she realized what the phantom shot had done; Syrin was supine, face up in a growing puddle of red. Markil crouched low over her, holding her head in his tiny hands. *No.* Celise felt herself shaking, willing the madness to stop. She felt fear bubbling to the top of her self; until all at once, the dark valley had vanished. Replacing it, the bright canyon was deafeningly active. She was lying behind a short boulder, her squad mates huddled around her. The air that had been so sweet in the night air returned to its wartime mixture of powder and fear.

"Cel! You plan on using that rifle yet?" Ata shouted at her between rifle bursts. Celise shook the strange vision that had carried her away, determination seeping in to take its place. Determination, until she peaked over the edge of the rock to see Talia horrifyingly still—the ground stained around her.

Darek's rough hands pulled her back behind cover just in time, and a round lodged itself in the rock. "If you aren't planning on joining us, just STAY DOWN!" he yelled, barely being heard over the cacophony of battle. Celise's mind was a whirlwind of activity. She realized, however, with a sort of detached thought, that she was still not moving. The din grew louder and louder, pressing in against her from all sides, until it felt as though the very air she breathed was trying to drown her. Far above the immediacy of direct combat, the whine of a gunship's engines began to creep ever closer to her senses. Celise noticed—somewhat strangely, she thought—that Rai, too, was hiding low against the rocks, just to one side of her.

The roaring scream of the ship grew more assertive, its efforts drowning out the closer staccato of rifle fire. Celise could feel her chest vibrating as the ground rumbled. Rai's head had raised slightly, and Celise looked into the deep mirror of fear that was etched across his face.

Ata was shouting something, probably something important, at least to her. The words didn't seem to mind what Ata wanted as they flickered away into the maelstrom of war. Darek had returned to her vision, and Celise's mind remarked at the odd expression it bore. He was clearly trying to say something; his mouth moved frantically. His arms flailed as he desperately tried to point at something just behind her. She felt her muscles flexing, her limbs moving seemingly unbidden; there was something rising past her fear. She turned over to see the sleek black form of the gunship high in the air, inching ever closer.

"Celise! The launcher! Now!" Darek's howling voice finally broke through the walls surrounding her consciousness. Her limbs were moving again, her hands grasped at the rugged metal cylinder she had been unwittingly pinning. Muscle memory took over completely as she felt the comfortingly familiar weight of the tube settling on her shoulder. As she sighted down the length of the weapon, aiming towards the cockpit of the black mass of terror, time seemed to contort in a wicked manner. She saw Syrin's face, then Markil's, then Talia's cruel mockery of slumber. Finally, she saw the gunship looming, its weapons hungry for blood.

Celise breathed in slowly, carefully, steadying her aim. She exhaled, a lifetime flashing past in the release of a single breath, and her finger tightened.

4

Enemy

17th of August, 2252
Three Days Later

*"Everyone is necessarily the hero,
of his own life story."*

Lyan's eyes were resting on her, she knew, but Celise had no interest in exerting the effort to raise her head. She was sitting down atop a crate of ammunition in an MDS operations base. They were far away from the action now, from the battle of Coprates Chasma. Still, inexplicably, her nose remained filled with the scent of violence. Her ears still pounded in her head, vehemently demanding to be liberated from their ringing. Her eyes retained their swell puff of smoke exposure.

Finally, it seemed Lyan had worked up the nerve to break their small bubble of silence. "What happened?"

It was a simple enough question, or at least it should have been. Celise lifted herself from the crate with reluctant resignation.

"It was an ambush." her voice sounded flat and distant, even to herself. "There was no amassing force, just a token garrison leading us to death." She paused, sucking in her breath sharply as a vicious image of Talia flashed across her mind. Lyan sat still, calmly waiting for her to continue.

"The enemy knew we were coming, there was no way out, and then the gunship arrived." As Celise kept recounting the events, she felt her strength returning, waves of resolve crashing into her. She closed her eyes and could smell the burning smoke of the wreckage.

"When the ship went down, it crashed into the enemy's position, but there was a survivor." As the last words escaped her lips, Lyan's eyes widened. Before he could respond, however, Captain Vayan was standing over them.

"Valen, Jure, with me!" His sharp, commanding voice seemed to shake Celise the last little bit she needed. She got quickly to her feet and marched alongside Lyan with a practised precision.

The pair followed Vayan into a command tent, where Lyan stumbled briefly as he took in the sight. In the middle of the tent, bound to a chair, was a haggard-looking young man in a tattered Commonwealth uniform. He was flanked by MDS guards, who briefly saluted the Captain's entry.

"This," began Vayan, "is 2nd Lieutenant Ezri Kanin of the Commonwealth's Special Services Group."

Celise and Lyan shared a brief look of apprehension. The SSG was a unit comprised of former Vanguard Special Forces members.

"He claims to have valuable intelligence that he will only deliver to someone 'not blinded by Martian pride.' It seems he's taken a shine to you, Jure."

Lyan took an involuntary half-step backwards at the mention. Then, recomposing himself, nodded dutifully, while trying to keep the uncomfortable look off his face. "I'll speak with him, sir."

Captain Vayan grunted an acknowledgement. "The rest of you, out. And Valen? Come with me."

As Celise followed along behind the Captain, her mind raced. This was no ordinary Loyalist soldier, nor were they a standard soldier of the Commonwealth. All of which meant that the enemy had clearly managed to slip past the Republic's space-based defences. She, likewise, was confounded by the man's strange request. Why Lyan? What was so special about him? Her mind continued to whirl as she reached the medical tent. Celise frowned; why here?

Captain Vayan gestured to one of the beds as he found himself a chair to pull up alongside. "Please," he implored, the earlier roughness trailing away from his voice. Celise was not so foolish as to deny the opportunity of rest wherever she could get it, not anymore, at least. The Captain's expression was one of worry, and kindness.

"Sir…" she began carefully, "what am I doing here?"

He smiled slightly, with just his eyes and one corner of his lips.

"I'd like you to tell me, Ensign Valen, what went wrong in that canyon." While his voice remained steady and his face calm, his words shook Celise something terrible. Seemingly sensing this, Vayan added, "Whenever you're ready, I understand there was an… incident, according to your squad mates."

Celise drew in three deep breaths successively in an effort to calm her still-active nerves. She tried to ignore the mixed feelings as she put her fragmented memory into words.

"I failed," Celise began simply, "I froze up, sir. Something happened when the fighting started. I couldn't move. I couldn't—" her voice escaped her grasp, pulling desperately out of reach. Vayan remained still, his eyes full of care, his gentle expression waiting patiently for her to return.

When she finally recaptured her words, she wished she hadn't. "I saw Syrin get shot. Even though I know it wasn't real, that it didn't really happen. Then, when I came back to reality, to the moment, Talia was just lying there; she wasn't moving—" Celise broke off once more, as the tears that had been welling in her eyes began to break past the dam.

The Captain nodded slowly, solemnly. "The stress of combat can do savage things to your mind, Ensign. I'm sorry to say it's not an uncommon thing to experience, especially as a new soldier."

A faint flicker of relief attempted to rise within Celise at his tone, but it was quickly crushed underneath the weight of guilt.

"Sir," she managed, "in my failure, I put my whole squad at risk. If Darek hadn't pulled me down when he did—"

"Stop," interrupted Vayan. "You're right." His voice was not unkind, but it held a renewed firmness. "Your actions, or rather your lack of action, could very easily have had severe consequences for your team."

Celise's eyes fell rapidly as shame cascaded over her.

"However, your failure need not define you. Not unless you let it." Vayan fixed her with a direct gaze now. "This is war, Valen, and you have a choice to make. You can let this failure break you, or you can rise above it, learn from it, and become a better soldier for it." The Captain stood, signalling the end of their conversation.

"Get some rest, Ensign. You'll need it for what's to come."

Lyan nearly walked straight into her as Celise was exiting the medical tent.

"Cel! There you are! Come with me, hurry!" Lyan's voice was shaking with some form of anticipation, his eyes wild and alight. Across the path, Ata hovered over some soldiers, glancing their way with distrusting eyes.

"What is it?" Celise managed as she allowed herself to be pulled along Lyan's urgent steps. "The prisoner," he breathed between footfalls, "Lieutenant Kanin. He told me something you need to hear."

As they approached the command tent, the pair of guards offered a curt nod as they allowed access. The prisoner, Ezri Kanin, was still seated in the same chair. He looked up as they approached, a flicker of recognition in his eyes.

"Lieutenant," Lyan started, "is this who—" The man's eyes stopped processing, having reached their destination.

"Celise Valen." The man spoke the acknowledgement with elite, clipped tones. His accent was so disorientingly Earthly that it took Celise a moment to recover.

"How do you know my name?" she questioned, her voice betraying her anxiety. The soldier smiled grimly. "Not yet, but soon. First, there are things you must know."

Celise felt the anger rising in her chest. This man was the enemy; this man was the reason her wife was in danger, the reason her son was gone!

Kanin seemed to be studying her, *reading* her. She turned away, hoping to cut him off from such ability.

"I'm sorry for your loss." His words buried themselves like daggers in her back. "It wasn't meant to happen like that."

"What do you mean?" Lyan asked, his confusion echoing her own. "The snipers." He said simply. "They were supposed to be holding fire, waiting until you were surrounded. Then the gunship was to emerge, and demand your surrender."

Celise turned back to the prisoner, steel eyes bearing down on him. "So? Why did they shoot?" Kanin held her gaze directly, unflinching. "Why does a soldier do anything? They received new orders. Orders they had come to rely on, orders from their supposed enemy."

Lyan was already halfway out the door, and Celise wanted desperately not to be left alone with this man. Until his eyes caught her once more and softened. Somehow, impossibly, the SSG lieutenant knew something of her, something real.

"Be well, Mrs. Valen."

Captain Vayan was speaking rapidly with Ensign Jure, their conversation hushed and urgent as Celise approached. One of the guards outside the command tent had pointed her in the right direction. The pair were standing near one of the camp's edges, on a rocky outcropping that overlooked the Eos valley.

"Thank you, Ensign, for bringing this to my attention." Celise heard Vayan say as she approached. The pair looked up as they noticed her.

"Ah, Valen, good. Ensign Jure here was just delivering some very valuable intelligence he says you helped extract from the prisoner. Well done."

"Oh?" Celise fumbled over her words momentarily, "That's kind of him to say, sir. Lyan really led the interview, though."

"Spoken well, Valen." He turned back to Lyan briefly, "Thank you for the update, Ensign. I suggest you rest up, you're dismissed." Lyan saluted quickly and marched toward his bunk.

Captain Vayan seemed to notice the worried expression on Celise's face, "Ensign Jure believes the prisoner was alluding to the presence of a spy in our ranks. Am I correct in understanding that you concur?" Celise straightened, adopting the attention stance. "Yes, sir. That is what we determined."

Vayan's gaze idled on her eyes a moment longer. "Well, no need for concern; I can assure you we will root out this traitor before long, certainly before you get back." His eyes smiled as he said this.

Celise frowned, "Back, sir?"

"You are being granted a leave of absence, Valen, one that comes with a well-earned promotion. Congratulations, Lieutenant."

5

Heart

14th August, 2252
Three Days Earlier

*"It's the possibility of having a dream come true,
that makes life interesting."*

The city streets were near-empty at the late hour. The reality of the war rarely brought itself to bear here, but people were still cautious. The long-coated man started walking again, confident he was not being followed. This was incorrect. The agent lying against the tree raised a hidden microphone to his lips.

"Target in seven," he murmured to the waiting operatives on the other end.

Seven seconds later, the shadows detached themselves from a wall next to long-coat. His mouth opened as though to scream or shout, and a swift blow hit the back of his head, silencing him.

Syrin sheathed her stun and, with the other operative's help, heaved his sleeping form into the freshly arriving vehicle. Finally, they collectively embarked themselves, and sped off into the night, leaving no trace of what had transpired.

The screen chimed, and a new mail made itself known to Syrin's eyes. Her heart jumped as she recognized the sender—Celise. With trembling fingers, she opened the message.

Syrin,

I hope this message finds you well, finds you safe. Things here are growing...difficult. This war is taking its toll on our people, and our planet, in ways I never imagined. Food is growing scarce, and the constant threat of attack hangs over us. I miss you terribly. Every day I wonder, are you safe, are you well. There's something else, you need to be careful, my love. There are rumours circulating here, about Earth-born citizens. Please be careful.

Always yours,

Celise.

Syrin's throat tightened as she closed the message, the traces of her wife fading with the light from the display. She worked hard to keep her face neutral as a group of other soldiers walked past her in the mess. The warning had her worried. She should have expected this of, course; it was the pattern of history. Still, to hear it confirmed by Celise was concerning all the same.

Picking up her meal, she moved into a common room to sit down somewhere more comfortable. On a couch, a group of soldiers were watching a broadcast attentively.

"...underground peace movements gaining traction in the outer colonies. The Martian Defence Service warns that such groups may be harbouring Commonwealth sympathizers and other spies. Citizens are encouraged to remain vigilant, and to report all suspicious activity."

Syrin turned briskly away from the group, feeling their eyes on her and sensing a new undercurrent in the room. She had to wonder, how long before her Earth origins were more widely known? And how long before they became a liability.

Three Days Later

"Major Valen, report to the Colonel's office, that's Major Valen to the Colonel." The radio chirped and went silent on Syrin's hip. With a sigh, she stood from behind her desk, powering down the systems. She straightened herself and pressed out any slight imperfections in her uniform, then opened the door from her cabin.

Syrin let out a small breath in relief. The hall was empty, at least for now. As she made her way along the starkly decorated passage, she passed by the numerous new board designs that were undergoing testing. They carried recruitment slogans. Some seemed well-thought-out, while others (such as the one showing an anthropomorphic red planet slowly vanishing) didn't.

Finally, she arrived at the door to Colonel Eglytis' office and knocked. The door slid open gracefully, bidding her entry.

Syrin crossed the threshold with one purposeful stride, coming to an attentive salute before the simple desk and its imposing occupant. The Colonel stood, gesturing easily to the chair opposite her desk.

"Please, Major. Be seated." The Colonel was an older woman, the former Marshal for the entire region, and Syrin's old commander. She took the seat offered. Colonel Eglytis studied her for what felt like a long time.

"How long have you been a member of the service, Major?" Syrin was briefly taken aback by the inquiry.

"Eight years, sir," she replied, her tone carefully calm. The Colonel nodded slowly, her face not betraying anything. "That's a long time. You've seen a lot of changes in that time, yes?"

Syrin studied her commander's face, searching for what wasn't there. "Yes, Colonel. Quite a bit." Eglytis leaned forward. "In all those years, Valen. You've served with distinction. Rising through the ranks despite your... challenges." Syrin stiffened, slightly, but remained silent.

"I am, of course, aware of your background," the Colonel continued, her voice getting softer. "Earth-born, married to a

Martian native. Your record is exemplary. That said, there are those within our ranks, and without, who perceive your origins as a liability."

Syrin's heart beat faster. The sounds of the hallway seemed to grow louder in her ears, and she had to work hard to keep her expression impassive. "With all due respect, I serve Mars dutifully, and I have never failed in my responsibilities. My loyalty is unwavering."

Colonel Eglytis leaned back, her expression softening. "I believe you, Syrin." A note of sadness crept into her words. "But we live in dangerous times—times when perception is everything." She pushed back from the desk and stood, turning to face a painting on her wall.

"Allegiances are being questioned, scrutinized even. Suspicion, is a powerful force." Eglytis stopped, turning back to face her confidant. "I've received disturbing reports, harassment, accusations of espionage, even violence." Syrin felt the cold of dread inch over her spine. "You are a valuable asset to the service, Major Valen." The Colonel sat once more, fixating Syrin with a direct gaze. "I have an assignment for you that, should you complete it, may alleviate some of the mistrust being directed towards you."

Major Valen sat up straighter in her chair and stilled her trembling vocal cords. "What are my orders, sir?"

Egyltis was perfectly still, her hands clasped together on the desktop. "We have identified a potential Commonwealth spy in our ranks who has recently stopped reporting in. You will find this traitor, Major Valen. Then you will eliminate him."

Three Days Later

Celise flicked open the panel on one side of the train car, dismissing the notification light. She wasn't far now, and had to keep from jumping at every sound, every potential incoming alert.

Celise,

> *Thank you for keeping up with the messages. I hope to see you again soon. Try not to spend too much time worrying about me; you'll never get anything done! I know the rumours are bad—I've heard plenty myself—but you must try to stay positive. In the end, I know everything will work out. We'll be okay—I know that. You have to know that, too.*

> *With love,*

> *Syrin.*

Celise kept looking over the message for many minutes after she had finished reading it. Finally, the train chimed a mournful alert, shaking her from her thoughts.

"Attention, travellers," the soft, mechanized voice spoke soothingly to its listeners. "Due to moving through a hot zone, we are temporarily extinguishing the lighting. Please return to your cabins and remain seated until the next announcement."

Celise closed the panel, dismissing the final vestige of light in her cabin. She turned to gaze out from the window, examining the dark, rocky landscape that stretched out before her. Somewhere, far away, out that window, she saw a flicker of illumination. Celise frowned slightly, squinting out at the darkness. Then, lamentably, she saw it clearly. There was a fire burning. First, just the one, then many, many more joined the affair. She watched, transfixed, as more and more dancers made themselves known. The elegant flames leapt up into the dark sky with reckless abandon, carefree in their destructive occasion.

She shuttered the window, snuffing out the dance of the dammed and resolving to obtain slumber.

Five Hours Later

The platform was stark, near empty. It was an unfortunate sight for Celise, who had finally grown accustomed to the bustling chaos of the capital. She made her way quickly across the open ground and towards the main road. She shivered, silently wishing she had brought something heavier than her uniform.

There were no cabbies waiting patiently by the station, and it was all the better to Celise's mind. The idea of a dedicated vehicle for a taxi was another strange Earth practice she never much cared for. Shouldering her belongings, she set out along the path, bound in the only direction she could think of.

The walk had a good distance to it, but nothing was truly ever that far away in a Martian city. After just over half an hour, she was stood still at the base of the steps to a place she didn't realize she feared so much. The house was still standing, still in order, remarkably untouched by the war. Celise stood in front of it, staring up at the door as though some hidden force was pushing her away.

At last, she defeated the mental spectre, stepped up the porch, and turned the handle. She was almost glad Syrin wasn't home yet. Almost.

Inside, she was struck by the invisible force carrying a wave of turbulent emotions. She set down her things and moved—almost subconsciously—to the counter. Keying for the water, she opened the cupboard to fetch a tea bag. The ritual she had practised so often lent her a small sort of comfort. A few minutes passed, and she was seated in her customary position, overlooking the yard through her favourite window. Celise didn't know how long she sat there, how long she waited in a quiet, contended sorrow.

At last, after many hours and a brief rest, Celise heard what she had been waiting for. The *tap, tap-tap, tap* that was the sound of Syrin's footsteps. The singularly impossible way she scraped the edge of the railing with her boot every time. Finally, the precise rhythm to her way of turning open the door handle. She was home.

The door creaked open, and Celise felt her heart skip more than a beat. Syrin stepped inside, and her eyes widened with shock and surprise.

"Cel?" she breathed, as if she did not dare believe it true. Wordlessly, Celise rose and crossed the room. She wrapped her wife in a tight embrace. They held each other close, worrying that the other might vanish if ever released.

Syrin whispered into her wife's shoulder, "I've missed you so much." Celise pulled away ever so slightly so that she might look deep into her eyes. Syrin's smile faltered slightly, "How did you get leave? Are you alright?" Her eyes swept down Celise's figure, scanning for any sign of apparent injury.

"I'm fine. Things are just... complicated, and I needed to see you." Syrin's eyes flicked down, and her smile returned slightly as she saw the signet. "Lieutenant?" she murmured with a raised eyebrow.

"I'm so proud of you." Celise finally allowed herself to smile and pulled her wife close.

Two Days Later

"Are you sure you have to go, Syr? We've had so little time..." Celise let her voice trail off; she knew the answer already.

"I'm sorry. This mission might finally clear me of suspicion." She was working hard to keep the pain out of her voice and the sadness out of her eyes. Of course, she needn't have bothered; Celise could read her like a book.

"I... I know. I just— Oh, I just *hate* this. This dammed war, the dammed Commonwealth, everything we've lost..." Celise clenched her fists tight, nails digging into her palms. Syrin squeezed her arm, gently.

"I know, Cel. I know, but we *must* keep going. For Mars, for each *other*." Celise drew in a deep, shuddering breath, nodding. Syrin smiled lightly and brushed a lock of straying hair from her wife's face. "I promise you, we will get through this, all of it. Together." Celise returned her smile, "Together," she echoed, her voice still just hairs past a whisper.

The small reprieve shattered into a thousand cries as a deadly wail cut through their home. The air raid sirens. Their eyes met, and in an instant, a flash of panic rushed through them.

"We need to move," Syrin said. She reached down and grasped Celise's hand, pulling her towards the door. "The shelter's not far."

The pair burst onto the street, and climbed aboard Syrin's waiting ride. The sky above was alight with the sounds and sights of battle. The badly outnumbered MDS Air Corps was buzzing with effort. They sped down the roadway as quickly as possible; Celise jumped as the first few explosions began to be heard. A dull thud in the distance that grew ever closer.

Arriving with haste at their destination, the two women leapt out towards the sanctuary. The ground shook beneath their feet as enemy explosives inched ever closer. Eventually, a weapon impacted close enough that they were showered with debris, and Syrin pulled Celise closer, shielding her with her body.

They rounded a final corner, and the entrance to the shelter was at last in sight. A few stragglers like themselves were hurrying inside, their faces contorted by the hand of fear. At last, Syrin and Celise were inside, and they huddled close at the base of a stairway. A booming roar of torment continued to scream its presence beyond their walls. Celise clung tightly to Syrin, the war would rage on outside, but for now, at that moment, they had each other. For now, it would have to be enough.

6

Truth

22nd of October, 2252
Three Months Later

"In war, truth is the first casualty."

Equal parts fear, and soot blanketed the small village. Celise felt the weight of war pressing down on her. Each step she took sounded impossibly loud in her ears. Her small team of Rai and Ata moved quickly, cautiously, around a ruined house. Celise raised one hand, signalling them to stop. She turned her head, straining to hear past the din of battle that was ongoing throughout the rest of the hamlet. The rest of the world faded away from her conscious mind, the presence overtaken by the faint footsteps of her enemy. She raised her rifle. The loyalist squad didn't have time to react before her team cut them down.

"Valen. Come in, Lieutenant Valen." Celise's radio crackled in her ear. "Repeat, Command to Va—" She depressed the small control to respond. "This is Valen; go ahead, Command." There was a brief pause from the other end of the line. "Valen, you are ordered to return to the square, maker four-oh, reinforce Ensign Shay's squad."

Celise took a moment to orient herself, then signalled Ata and Rai to start moving out. "Copy," she acknowledged on the radio. "En route."

The team moved with deadly grace through the narrow, rubble-strewn streets towards the centre of town. Rolling, ricocheting echoes of gunfire and explosions grew louder, and more oppressive. The billowing clouds of jet-black smoke grew closer, and each breath Celise took felt harsher than the last.

Finally reaching their target, the group surveyed a scene of utter devastation. What had once been a vibrant town square lay in ruins, pockmarked by craters and littered with debris. Celise blinked away a snap-vision of Markil. He had grown up in a town not dissimilar to this. She had grown her family there. She had—

Ensign Shay's shout cut through the fog to reach her.

"Lieutenant! Glad you could make it!" he yelled over the gunfire before covering again as more rounds impacted the small wall he was huddled behind. That wall was crumbling, and Celise knew it was only a matter of time before someone took it out. She peered out cautiously from behind her own corner-cover. The loyalists had fortified themselves on the upper storey of an old block of units.

Celise looked over her shoulder to Rai. "Line up on that doorway!"

He nodded, crouched down, and sighted his rifle on the bottom level of the building.

"Ata, space," she commanded, and Sorensen dutifully moved next to Rai to allow her Lieutenant room for manoeuvring.

Celise pulled off the long, cylindrical device from her back. Deadly memories swam into her sight, threatening to pull her into a slumber. She shook her head violently and shouldered the launcher. Pausing to take careful aim at one of the remaining second-storey supports, she sucked in her breath, and fired.

The effect was immediate, and as desired. The building's frame collapsed, leaving little standing above the ground level. Almost a minute passed, and then she saw the figures. Slow-moving, a group of loyalists emerged from the rubble. Their faces were coated in dust and blood. Their eyes were wide and full of horror. Their bodies were beaten, limbs twisted.

Rai and Ata stood up, moving to her side. Shay's squad quickly got to their own feet, weapons trained on the enemy survivors. Celise counted four of them, with no weapons that she could see. Shay's team held their tracks.

"On your knees!" the Ensign barked, "hands in plain sight!" The fighters hesitated. Hesitated for just a moment too long.

The rippling crack of rifles rolled from Shay's squad to Celise's ears. Rai flinched. Celise and Ata didn't.

She watched as the line of four toppled over, dispatched with clinical efficiency. A caustic scent clung to the air surrounding Celise. Equal parts smoke, blood, and resignation filled the air of the centre, trying desperately to choke the occupants. She felt her eyes lingering, staring really at the bodies crumbled in dust. Their final expressions were simple, and all-captivating. Fear, confusion, and pain rolled into one and etched into their faces.

Celise felt something cold, hollow, and barren settling in her heart. A feeling she had grown accustomed to, to the point of it almost lending her comfort.

"The area is secure, Lieutenant," Ensign Shay spoke into her mind. His voice was practical, devoid of feeling. Celise nodded curtly and tore her gaze away from the corpses.

"Good work, Ensign," she replied mechanically, the words coming to bear automatically. "Set up a perimeter, prepare for a counter-assault."

As the soldiers of her command made themselves busy carrying out her new orders, she found a quiet corner out of the way to collect herself. The battle hadn't been long, but that hadn't dampened its brutality. A memory drifted, unbidden, into her thoughts: her days of training, Ata helping her when she was injured, Darek goofing off. Now she looked up, and took in the devastation.

"Is this the beauty of victory?" she wondered aloud. A commotion from one side of the square drew her attention. A group of civilians were being escorted in a line across the street. One of them stumbled, and Ata kicked at them roughly.

"Move it, scum!" she yelled at the trembling man. His face was contorted with fear, but his eyes had nothing to show at all. Celise felt something, like a small voice within, pleading for attention. She felt confused, unsure of what was happening. Suddenly, she realized she was storming towards Ata, her legs seeming to have made a decision for her.

"Sorensen!" she barked, her voice coming out clear, authoritative, despite her internal strangeness. "Stand down. Now." Ata stopped mid-assault, spinning to face Celise. Her face was a mask of surprise and, Celise thought, resentment.

"These people are collaborators! They've been feeding and sheltering the enemy!" Ata retorted. Celise noticed with a flicker of panic that the Ensign's hand was holding the butt of her gun. Celise pushed a dark, sharper tone into her voice. "You've been given an order, Ensign. You *will* comply."

Celise noticed abruptly that Darek and his small team were watching from one side of the street. They looked tense.

Ata glared at her for a long minute. A time throughout which the air seemed electrified by the menace of bloodshed. Celise stood her ground, her eyes locked with Ata's, until, at last, the Ensign dropped her gaze to the ground.

"Yes sir," she spat, her voice barely containing fury.

Nine Hours Later

The hum of the transport's engines had long since faded into the background of Celise's mind. She gazed in silence out the small, porthole window. Travelling across the once elegant landscape now scarred by battle brought thoughts of terror back to her mind.

Rai shifted uncomfortably in his seat across from her. With his voice dry, he broke the hours-long silence.

"Lieutenant, I don't understand. Why are we pulling back? The fighting isn't exactly letting up on the front." Celise shuttered her eyes tightly, enabling them to re-target Rai without distractions.

She sighed heavily, opening her eyes again. "I don't know much more than you do, Rai. We're being redeployed for some kind of classified operation, but they wouldn't tell me anything else."

Ata snorted derisively. "Classified? Yeah, right. We're grunts, Valen. That stuff's a job for special forces, not the fodder."

"That's enough, Ensign," Celise snapped, silencing Sorensen's comments. She half-parted her lips a moment, then seemed to think better of it.

Celise leaned back against the headrest and closed her eyes once more. She didn't much understand the abrupt orders herself. After months at the front, day after day of brutal combat, to be yanked away was jarring. The incidents of the village square gnawed at her, an uneasy feeling settling in her gut. Her conscience felt like it was being hammered against from all sides simultaneously. Celise mentally stepped through the incidents that had been growing more and more frequent. Her memory drifted back to when she had just returned from leave.

Three Months Earlier

Celise thanked the guard at the primary gate and moved across it into the camp. The base was abuzz with activity, to the point where nobody was paying her much attention. She surveyed the zone, identifying quickly the junior officer's barracks and setting out towards it. As she walked, she couldn't stop thinking about Syrin. They'd had so little time back together, and there was still so much Celise had wanted to do, wanted to say.

She stepped out of her mental wanderings when she arrived at the barracks and scanned the list for her name and bunk number. When she had finished unpacking, she straightened her uniform, and made for the general mess. As she missed Syrin, she too had missed her squad, her team. Rai, Ata, Darek, and Lyan were as close to friends as could be found out here.

The mess was alight with the chattering sounds of camaraderie. Celise's eyes scanned the room until finally spotting Ata and Rai seated at the end of a long table. As she approached, Rai took notice of her.

"Lieutenant!" he called out to her, his face warming into a smile. "Welcome back!" Celise returned his smile, only partially having to force it, and took a seat across from him, shouldering Ata. "Good to see you two again."

Ata looked up, nodding curtly. "Valen," she acknowledged. Celise looked around, eyes sweeping the assembly for the faces she was missing. "Where's Lyan? Darek?" she asked, arranging her tray in front of her.

Ata's fork paused mid-movement, hovering just shy of its target. Rai's eyes darkened in shadow. The pair exchanged a quick look. Ata set down the cutlery, and Rai spoke. "Darek's in the infirmary. He... got hit pretty bad on the last patrol."

Celise felt her heart start to sink. She drew in a deep, quiet breath. "Is he going to make it?"

Rai nodded slowly and carefully. "Some of the docs think so. Others... aren't so sure."

Celise let out the breath she had been holding. "And... Lyan? What about him?" She almost didn't want to push, fearing what she may hear.

Ata stiffened, sitting up even straighter, as a haunted, hollow gaze filled Rai's eyes. Ata's voice was cold, clipped when she answered. "Gone." Celise felt a chill creep along her spine and turned to face Sorensen. "Gone? What do you mean 'gone'? Where is he?" she demanded.

Her words didn't seem to register with Ata, who returned to mindlessly picking at the food on her tray. Rai shifted. "We don't exactly know," he began, "Lyan was called in for questioning just shortly after you left. We, uh, haven't seen him since."

Celise felt her mind reeling. "What?" That was all she managed to say right away. "Lyan... Wait, haven't you asked about him?" She realized, belatedly, that her tone carried a note of accusation.

Ata narrowed her eyes. "It. Doesn't. Matter." There was a harshness, a fear to her words, that Celise hadn't seen before. "The *officers* have made their decision. We follow orders, *Lieutenant.* I suggest you remember that." With her final remark, Ata stood and marched hastily away.

Rai caught Celise's eye. "She's been through a lot. We all have, I guess. You missed, well you missed quite a bit, Lt."

Celise nodded. "I know, I'm sorry I wasn't here."

Rai's expression softened. "You're here now," he said simply.

Celise tried to offer up a small smile, but it felt wrong, somehow. "Tell me everything," she started. "I need to know what I've missed."

Three Months Later

The transport shook, jolting Celise out of her memory. Her eyes snapped open as the transport lurched, coming to a stop. She blinked, briefly feeling disoriented, as reality reasserted itself. The rear doors hissed open, revealing the bustling life that was a forward operations base.

Celise stood from her seat near the now-open doors. "Attention!" she commanded, and the rows of soldiers quickly got to their feet, forming two neat lines. "Dis-mount!" she called, and the troops started disembarking, two-pair, until she was the last one.

As she stepped out, and emerged into the cool Martian air, she couldn't shake the feeling that something was wrong. The classified op, the abruptness of their redeployment—it all spoke to something big at play. A young soldier hurried up to her front.

"Lieutenant Valen? The Colonel has requested your presence, sir." Celise returned the fighter's salute, then turned to Rai and Ata. "I'll link up with you two later." Rai nodded, his face quizzical, and moved away. As she walked, Celise felt her mind threatening to run away from the situation once again. Every step took her closer to answers, and she wasn't sure she wanted them.

The Colonel's office was spartan—barely more than a chair and table, really—and its occupants were dressed in starkness. Captain Vayan stood off to the side, his face grim, as he offered her a brief nod of welcome.

"Lieutenant Celise Valen, reporting as ordered," she stated promptly, assuming attention.

The Colonel, with the name placard "Eglytis," looked up. "At ease, Lieutenant."

She relaxed her posture.

"What I have to tell you today is of the utmost secrecy. It does *not* leave this room. Am I understood?"

Her gaze was piercing enough to melt steel, Celise thought, and she took some small pride in not looking away.

"Yes, sir," she affirmed. "What are my orders?"

Colonel Eglytis exchanged a look with Vayan before speaking. "We have reliable intelligence, which suggests there is a highly placed Commonwealth operative inside the MDS. Your objective is to capture this individual, and bring them in for interrogation."

Celise felt the look of confusion that splayed across her face. "Understood, Colonel. If I may ask, however, why isn't my team with me? Is this a solo operation?"

Captain Vayan addressed her, "The team has already been briefed. You won't be leading your standard squad this time, Valen. We'll be having you insert with a team from Wolf Brigade."

The Colonel was staring hard at her, appraising her. "You have questions, Lieutenant." It wasn't posed as a question, simply an acknowledgement of fact.

Celise felt her cheeks burn slightly. "No, sir. I understand the assignment. Who's the target?"

Captain Vayan's gaze shifted down, looking intently at the floor. Eglytis didn't flinch as she delivered the devastating name.

"Major Syrin Valen."

Celise felt her world tilting, spinning, threatening to careen out of control. She gripped one hand against a wall, abandoning all pretense of control. The Colonel's words echoed in her mind, over and over, sounding louder and louder.

"That's not possible," she heard herself say, not sure how she had spoken. Her voice was very far away from her ears; so far, it sounded like someone else. "There—There must have been some mistake," she managed.

Captain Vayan looked up, his eyes wells of stern sympathy, "I'm afraid not. The evidence is quite clear, Celise. Major Valen has been passing on sensitive information to loyalists for months now."

Celise's mind was racing, scrambling, panicking. She thought of the recent strangeness of deployments, the odd gaps in her wife's messages. She thought, at last, about the growing suspicion towards any Earth-born citizen. This last thought, briefly, brought to mind Lyan.

"I don't… I don't understand," she managed to breathe out, regaining some semblance of composure. "Why me?"

The Colonel leaned back, studying her with a practised eye. "Put simply," she began, "you know the target. Your connection makes you uniquely aware of her patterns, habits, and weaknesses."

She sat forward again. "Moreover, it will prove *your* loyalty beyond any doubt."

The implication was clear: This was no mission. It was a test. The weight of the world seemed to press down upon her, threatening to crush her into nothingness. She thought of her duty, her love, and the brutality she had both borne witness to and participated in. She thought of the village, of Ata, of the lines of prisoners outside awaiting their fate.

Celise shut her eyes tight, trying in vain to block out the universe. She breathed slowly, deeply, centring herself. When at last her eyes opened once more, determination took hold in them.

"I understand, sir. When do I leave?"

Celise inhaled. It was what felt like the first full breath since she had entered the command room. She spotted Rai across the main path; he was walking towards her, his pace brisk.

"L-T!" he called out. "There's someone that wants to see you."

Celise frowned in slight confusion.

"Remember that Commonwealth prisoner you spoke with?"

Celise had to rack her memory a moment before recalling, "Lieutenant Kanin? The SSG operative?" Rai nodded. "He's asking for you for some reason."

The guards resumed their posts as Celise and Rai entered the small prison chamber. Ezri Kanin, 2nd Lieutenant in the Commonwealth's Special Services Group, sat on the cot in one corner of the room. He looked up as they entered, and Celise thought she saw a faint smile on his lips.

"Valen, Celise. 26th June, Capital District, son." The SSG soldier spoke quickly, his tone commanding the room in its entirety.

Celise took a half-stumbling step back. "How—"

The word had barely left her mouth when the man spoke again. "Now that I have your attention, I believe it is time to speak freely with the both of you. The Commonwealth of Sol is *not* your enemy. You"—he pointed at Celise—"must move quickly if you are to save Syrin."

Celise took a step toward him, equal parts anger, confusion, and fear rising up in her. Rai caught her by the arm, steadying her, pulling her back.

"Explain," he addressed the prisoner tersely. Kanin held his hands up, palms out, in front of him. "I understand the confusion. Allow me to clear things up for you. All SSG operatives being dispatched to Mars were given the task of memorizing a set of people. Individuals in the MDS that we may encounter, and who may not understand why they are truly fighting."

Celise's fists clenched tightly, and it took every fibre of her being not to lunge at the man. She gritted her teeth instead. "Go on."

"Thank you," the man started. "First off—the attack on the governor's declaration speech? The one that kicked off this whole mess of a war? It wasn't us. It was staged, all of it, to give an excuse for the war. The Martian Government instigated the entire thing; their list is our own. You were on it, Celise. You were known, from the beginning, to be one who would join up with fervour."

For what felt like the hundredth time in recent memory, Celise felt her world collapsing. It wasn't true; she pressed herself to believe. After all, it simply couldn't be, not if she wanted to keep living, keep serving.

After a moment, Rai nodded to the prisoner to continue. "I'm sorry, for everything you've gone through here. More will suffer unless we *act*."

Celise breathed, deeply, completely, trying desperately to still her beating heart. For what felt like hours, the room was silent, devoid of all but the faintest of hums from the walls. Finally, Celise fixed Ezri with a direct gaze.

"What do I do?" The question sounded faint; it sounded like weakness to her own ears. It sounded like her.

Kanin straightened the clothes he was wearing, his fingers moving to smooth out tiny bumps and creases. "I'm going to be executed tomorrow." His words carried a finality to them; there was no wondering, no uncertainty, nothing but cold truth.

"That," he continued, "will be your opportunity. You need to get away from here, as far as you can. I'll provide you with a set of coordinates. Go there, and you'll meet up with a loyalist faction that knows about you. Your code word will be *Pavonis*."

Rai hadn't moved, hadn't spoken, Celise thought maybe hadn't breathed even, in a long time. "I'm with you, Lt. All the way," he said with confidence, a tone that barely contained his fear.

7

Crossroads

23rd of October, 2252
One Day Later

"Do not go gentle into that good night.
Rage, rage against the dying of the light."

Celise walked with purpose alongside Rai towards the wall. The yard was quiet, eerily still so early in the morning. She felt the weight of her rifle on her shoulder. The weapon's hard form felt as though it had meshed with her own over the course of countless battles. She turned her head as they marched and matched Rai's sad smile with her own.

Then, for the benefit of those in the square—namely the Captain and Colonel—she spoke at a raised volume to her charge.

"Move it, prisoner!" She tried to put some vile into her voice as she spoke to Lieutenant Kanin, aided by glancing at Eglytis before saying it. Her facade hung in the air, and as the trio approached the wall, thin rays of sunlight began to peek above the horizon.

Kanin walked calmly, head held high, between them. Celise and Rai marched in perfect synchronization. "Halt!" Celise commanded, coming to a stop flawlessly alongside Rai. Kanin turned so that his back was to the wall, his visage perpendicular to the concrete telegraph of fate. Rai and Celise executed an about-turn, and marched into position at the firing line, turning then to face the condemned man.

Celise realized that Ata was here; she was not far away, her rifle slung over her shoulder. Captain Vayan and Colonel Eglytis were positioned opposite Sorensen, their faces masks devoid of any emotion—unreadable. A young Ensign beside the Captain said something, and Vayan nodded, motioning to Eglytis.

"Present arms!" Ata shouted the first command. Celise and Rai moved with practised precision, unslinging rifles and holding them out across their chests. Celise inhaled slowly, blinking long before the next command. "Make ready!" Ata called.

Celise and Rai responded as ordered, moving as one. Celise felt mechanical as her hand snapped up to the bolt of her rifle. She pulled it back, then snapped it into place, chambering a single round of ammunition. Celise exhaled, and Colonel Eglytis took a step forward.

"Second Lieutenant Ezri Kanin of the Commonwealth of Sol." She announced his title for the benefit of the MDS-required recording devices present. "You have been found guilty of espionage against the Republic of Mars. The punishment for this crime, is death."

Kanin continued standing tall, and unwavering, eyes front. He wasn't looking at her, Celise knew, though it felt like it.

"Do you have any final words?" The Colonel offered the final formality. The Lieutenant remained silent, and still. Eglytis nodded curtly and stepped back alongside the... Captain? Celise noticed with a start that the Captain wasn't there! Her mind raced, about to panic, and she breathed deeply in an attempt to settle herself. Ata stepped up again.

"Take aim!" The third order hit Celise from the side as a shock impact. She knew, this had to go perfectly to plan. She raised her rifle, side by side with Rai. They both settled the stock of the weapon into their shoulders, leaning forward, and sighting their *target* as instructed. Celise drew in her breath, relaxed her muscles, and prepared herself for the final moment—the final chance.

"Fire!" As Ata's shout rippled out across the yard, Rai and Celise sprang into action. Celise spun to her left abruptly, bringing her rifle's sights to bear on Ata's chest. Simultaneously, Rai spun to his right, aiming to sight the Colonel. At least, that should have been what happened, if all had gone to plan.

For Celise, time slowed to a crawl as she completed her turn. Instead of a look of surprise on Ata's face, there was only anger. Celise's eyes widened in shock as she realized the woman's rifle was already trained on her. In a fleeting moment, Celise knew that she had failed. That her plan had failed, and that she would not escape. She did not think for long, however, before Darek's rough form bowled her over, tackling and pinning her to the ground, his own sidearm now in her face.

"Traitor!" he screamed, face awash with rage. Celise didn't hear what he said next, as a single gunshot overwhelmed her ears. She wriggled free just enough to see Ata lowering her rifle, unfired. Celise twisted her head and stared in disbelief and sorrow at Rai's still form, a dark stain blossoming on his chest. Captain Vayan was standing over him, over *it*, smoke trailing from the barrel of his weapon. She stopped moving and knew her body had gone limp.

"You disappoint me, Valen." Her Captain's words stung more than she had expected them to as he approached, and knelt on one knee to her side. "We could have done *great* things together." He shook his head, a cruel mask of sadness overtaking it.

Eglytis' voice carried over from her calm, watchful position. "Get her up," she commanded, and Darek began dragging Celise into a kneeling position. "Her work's not finished yet." Only now did the Colonel's face change form at all, to a cruel smile. Celise felt her body being shifted until her head was pulled back to look down the line to the wall. Ata was standing in front of her now, with her rifle trained on Kanin.

"I'm sorry," he mouthed, and then the round cut him down.

Celise knelt, unmoving, in the dusty courtyard; her world shattered once more. The blood of her friend stained the ground next to her, and her only source of the truth lay slumped against the far wall. She had failed them both, failed herself.

Celise smelled the gunpowder in the air, felt Darek's iron grip holding her in place, and saw the tears welling up in her own eyes. She knew, too well, what the price for her actions would be. She thought of Syrin, and thought of how she would never, ever again, see her wife. The cost of war, all at once, felt impossibly high.

Vayan stepped in front of her, partially obscuring her view of Kanin's lifeless form. His face spoke of disappointment, and his lips mirrored the sentiment. "I had such high hopes for you, Valen. Now, you've thrown it all away. For what? For Commonwealth *scum*?" He lowered his head to look directly into her eyes, as his voice grew quiet. "These are the people that killed your *comrades*, your *friends*, your *family!*"

Celise glared back at his eyes, somewhere finding a source of defiance she didn't realize she could. "I chose the *truth*," she spat.

"Truth?" Vayan roared. "What in the moons does truth have to do with anything! This is *war*, Valen!" Celise matched his fury with her own. "I shouldn't expect *you* to understand. You all abandoned truth a long time ago."

The Captain raised a hand at once, as though to strike her when Colonel Eglytis' knife-like voice cut through the air. "Enough. We're not done with her." Vayan lowered his hand and stood, regaining his composure. Eglytis' horrid imitation of a smile returned. It took on a new form, a cold, predatory appearance that chilled Celise to her core.

"The Lieutenant still has one last mission to complete. Isn't that right, Mrs. Valen?" The gnawing pain of realization dawned on Celise. They were still planning on capturing Syrin.

"Never!" She struggled against Darek's firm grip. "I'll never help you hurt her!" The Colonel's smile only grew in response.

"Oh?" she mused, seemingly enjoying the interaction very much. "I think you will. One way or another."

Celise felt every fibre of strength within her building; her muscles tensed as instincts took over. She prepared herself to lunge at the Colonel, the consequences be damned. Before she had a chance, a thunderous explosion rocked the base. Alarms blared, and smoke billowed from a nearby building, from the building where Kanin had been held.

Celise saw her chance and knew she wouldn't soon get another. She jabbed backward fiercely with her elbow, knocking Darek off her, and the breath out of him. As he doubled over, Celise rolled, snatching up his fallen sidearm. Ata had almost completely turned around now, the momentary distraction of the blast over for her. She wasn't quick enough. Celise fired twice, two shots in quick succession that sent Ata sprawling to the ground in a cry of pain.

She scrambled to her feet, firing wildly behind her as she ran towards the transport section. Gunfire was erupting sporadically from around the camp now. Disoriented, freshly woken, and confused soldiers ran out of their spaces, unsure of what was happening. Celise reached a ground transport, and clambered aboard, gunning the engine before slamming shut the armoured door. She heard the pings of rounds off the hull, and she hit down hard on the accelerator. The vehicle rammed past the gate, and she was free.

Celise wasn't sure how long she had been driving for, but it was at least over an hour. At last, the engine shut off abruptly, and Celise kicked the inside hull in dismay. Sighing, she opened the door, and disembarked onto the ground below. As soon as she planted her feet, she felt them threaten to give out. Steadying herself against the transport door, she looked down, and saw the red splotch that was staining her side. Sitting down, she inspected the wound, and breathed a sigh of relief. The round hadn't penetrated, just grazed her. She tore off a piece of her uniform's sleeve, feeling a small sense of grim joy in the action, and tied it around herself.

She sank to her knees in the dust. Her body trembling in a fictional cold, fabricated by exhaustion, pain, and sorrow. The stolen transport's charge was depleted, abandoned behind her. With an effort belying the action, she raised her head, eyes looking out across the red horizon. The events of the past few hours played over and over in her mind, some horrible nightmare she could not awake from. Yet, she realized she wasn't sure she wanted to. She had to remember, had to *know*. For all those who could not.

"I'm sorry," she whispered to the ghosts that would listen. "I'm so sorry. For all of it." Her voice cracked, and she slowly got to her feet, blinking away the tears that wanted to seize her vision. She didn't blame them; they only wanted to protect her from reality. Celise knew she didn't have long, couldn't stay in one place. The MDS was sure to be hunting her extensively, and she was vulnerable out here in the open. With a grit of determination, she forced herself to take the first step. Then, biting back the pain, she took the next.

As she trudged along her chosen path, perpendicular to the road, her thoughts, as they often did, turned to Syrin. Her heart felt like a lead weight in her chest. An aching fear threatened to drown her if she paid it too much attention. She had been branded a traitor. Not just branded, she knew. She *was* a traitor, by its very definition. She couldn't help it, worrying about Syrin. Would they try to use her? To force her to help them? She couldn't imagine it. Celise longed, desperately, to hold Syrin close again. To tell her everything, to understand the truth. For now, however, such a reunion seemed a universe away.

The sun beat down mercilessly on Celise as she walked; her legs threatened to give way with every step. Her throat was parched, her head laden, but she refused to give up. Ezri's words echoed in her mind: "The Commonwealth is not your enemy." It was true, she knew. Because, in order for her to go on, it had to be. She would find a way, some way, to expose the lies. Some way to bring down the true betrayers, and to finally end this senseless war. She owed it, after all. For Kanin, for Rai. For Lyan, for Talia. For Markil. She owed it too, she knew, to Darek, Ata, and all those swept up in this horrible game. She owed them, perhaps most of all, the pawns.

Fifteen Hours Later

The light began to fade as the sunset encroached ever nearer. Celise's legs felt as though they could go no further, and she breathed a sigh of relief when she saw a small, rocky outcropping. It wasn't much, but it would have to do as a shelter for the night. She found the strength to quicken her pace, eager for rest.

As she neared the rocks, a figure emerged slowly from behind them. Celise felt her heart leap into her throat. Instinctively, she drew her sidearm, the adrenaline momentarily stopping the shaking of her hand.

"Don't move!" she called out to the spectre, drawing aim on the target almost automatically. The shadow raised its hands slowly, standing perfectly still.

"Cel," she spoke. "It's me." Celise squinted through the light, not daring to believe her battered ears. Then she saw her, the face of her love, Syrin. She stepped cautiously forward, concern on her face.

"Syr?" Celise whispered, hoping not to shatter the illusion with her voice. She lowered the gun, as Syrin moved forward quicker. "How—how did you find me?" she managed to choke out through the tears she could no longer keep at bay.

Syrin finally closed the distance, taking the weapon gently from Celise's now trembling hands. "I heard through the wire you had fled, been deemed traitor. I figured I had better find you first." A small smile danced onto her lips.

Celise felt a surge of joy, then an overwhelming ache of tiredness. She collapsed into her wife's arms, overcome by the pain and exhaustion of her journey. Syrin held her closely, stroking her hair gently.

"It's okay, Hun. It's alright. Everything will work out. I've got you; you're safe."

8

Hope

27th of October, 2252
Three Day Later

*"There is some good in this world,
and it's worth fighting for."*

In the days following their reunion that night, Celise and Syrin mainly spent healing and partly moving their temporary hideouts from place to place. For the time being, they were huddled together against a rock, under the cool night sky. A small fire burned brightly and fiercely in front of them.

Celise gazed up into the dark abyss, transfixed, and murmured softly, "If stars could cry... would they weep for us?"

Syrin blinked her eyes open slowly and looked at her wife with a quizzical concern. "What was that?" she asked, her voice tired and low.

Celise smiled up at her lightly. "Sorry, didn't mean to wake you. Just something a poet friend of mine once wrote. 'Would the stars cry for us?' I don't know what brought it to me."

Syrin's face adopted a thoughtful smile, and she followed Celise's gaze to the sky. "I think they would," she replied. It was cold, colder than usual, and Celise could see her wife's breath as moisture in the air when she spoke. Syrin rolled onto one knee and reached for her bag.

"We'd better keep moving; it shouldn't be much further now. You're sure the coordinates are right?" Her voice carried more disbelief than she had intended, and Celise frowned.

"As sure as I can be, and anyway, it's not like we've got much in the way of choices right now."

They had been moving, as far as they could manage, towards the location Lieutenant Kanin had given Celise. Syrin looked worried, but then, Celise hadn't seen many other expressions recently.

"Why?" she asked, her heart beginning to move faster. Syrin's eyes were searching the horizon as though there was something more to see than the endless rocks and dust.

"It's probably nothing; maybe I'm just reading the map wrong." Celise let out a short, humourless laugh. "You? Come on, what's the matter?"

Syrin finally drew her gaze back to her wife. "Well, if those coordinates *were* correct, and if the map is too... We should be practically on top of the loyalist camp." Celise heard a voice from within. Far away, at the back of her mind, a tiny voice of panic was beginning to call out.

"Okay," she managed after a few long breaths. "That could mean a lot of things." Syrin kicked some dust over the smouldering fire, snuffing out the remnant flames. "Maybe," she started, "they've simply moved."

Celise started nodding slowly. "We've seen no signs of battle here. There would be marks if they'd been overrun." Syrin was looking over her map again, tracing invisible lines with her fingers.

"Where would they have gone..." she mumbled. Celise stepped to her side, her own eyes starting to scan the layout of their world, when at last she saw it.

"Pavonis!" Celise exclaimed. There was a small overshelf at the base of Pavonis Mons, and it was one of the closest places to take shelter from their current position.

Syrin looked her in the eye, appraising carefully. "You're certain?" Celise nodded with fervour, picking up her own bag. "*Pavonis* was the code phrase Ezri gave me. That's where they've gone."

Syrin nodded and oriented the map so that they could plot a walking route.

Two Hours Later

It hadn't taken them long to start seeing signs of their destination. The winds had been calm, and despite the darkness, it was getting easier to see the occasional track or discarded item. The latter used to make Celise's stomach churn. That was before the war when she'd had the luxury of caring. Still, barely audible, a small sigh of disappointment made itself known.

Suddenly, Syrin came to a stop. They could see the overshelf now, one side of it anyway. Celise stopped walking, trusting her wife's instincts, and waiting for her to voice them.

"Celise," she began, her voice steady, still, calm, yet with a slight note of tension. "Copy my movements, exactly."

Syrin slowly moved her hands outwards, away from her sides, so they hung awkwardly, away from her waist. Celise frowned with slight confusion but followed carefully. Syrin then slowly raised her arms higher. She placed them together at the back of her head, where she interwove her fingers.

Celise felt the dawning of realization as she copied the motion. Evidently, her wife had noticed something—or, more accurately, someone—whom she'd personally missed.

Syrin opened her mouth and spoke at a raised volume. "My only weapon is the pistol you can see in its holster." She kept very still as she said this, and Celise had a horrible feeling that somewhere, a weapon was trained on them.

"We have come under the direction of 2nd Lieutenant Ezri Kanin of the SSG." She turned her head, very slowly, and deliberately, to Celise.

Celise took the prompt and spoke at a high volume. "My only weapon is a sidearm; it is in the bag on my shoulder." She decided to start the same way. "Kanin gave us coordinates to find you and the code phrase *Pavonis*."

She looked out at the rocks and sparse topography. Her eyes searched frantically for whoever was out there, whoever was watching. At last, a movement caught her eye. A shadow detached itself from a rock to her left. Celise's breath caught in her throat at how *close* they were. The figure stood, revealing the camouflage suit that had blended so seamlessly with the surface.

Syrin and Celise remained carefully still as the figure approached, careful not to make any sudden moves. The warrior stopped before reaching them. While their face was hidden behind a visor, it was evident that the newcomers were being appraised.

The soldier lifted one arm and pointed at Syrin. "Remove your weapon," came the sleek, helmet-modulated voice.

Syrin nodded and complied slowly. She moved her left arm down from her head. Then, she reached across her body to the pistol's grip and removed it slowly using her index finger and thumb. She bent slightly, depositing the weapon at her feet, before resuming her earlier stance.

The soldier seemed satisfied with this and pointed next at Celise. "Drop the bag," was the following command. Celise complied, carefully manoeuvring her right arm so that the bag would drop off her shoulder carefully.

The watching loyalist waited only a moment after to turn around completely. "Follow." Celise and Syrin slowly lowered their weary arms to their sides. They turned slightly and saw that two more camouflage operatives were behind them. Exchanging a look of resignation-tinged hope, they set off behind their guide.

A large boulder—presumably mounted on some sort of rail—slid seamlessly to one side, revealing the encampment's entrance. As they had gotten closer, Celise and Syrin had noticed more of the camouflage sentries, intermittently placed along their route. Inside, the encampment was settled into the vast, cavernous formation. About the makeshift base, people sat, walked, and talked in military dress—with the occasional civilian attire poking through. Through the voices and accents, Celise picked out a number of Earth and Martian natives. There were also a few she couldn't quite place, but at a guess, they would have been from the outer colonies.

Syrin shared a glance with her, seeming to echo her own thoughts. Volunteers, citizens of the Commonwealth, really had come from all across the system to fight. It was, for Celise, as shocking as it was humbling. A flag draped, from its attachment to the high rock ceiling. The black-red-black banner had been her target, her enemy, the source of all her hatred. *No.* She corrected herself. It was not the source, merely where the hate was directed.

The escort removed their helmet, revealing a man with close-cropped hair and kind, haunted eyes. "I'm Captain Reeves of the Commonwealth Ground Forces," he introduced himself curtly, with only a minor note of bitterness creeping in. Celise noticed his accent was significantly modulated, not so far from the films she'd seen of Triton. "We've been expecting you, though I admit not quite like this."

Syrin's posture straightened as she took a single step further. "Major Syrin Valen, formerly of the Martian Defence Service. This," she gestured to her side, "is my wife, Lieutenant Celise Valen."

The Captain nodded, his expression softened slightly. "We were hoping to hear from you sooner; the defection has caused quite a stir." He paused, seeming to study the pair for a few more moments. "I take it Kanin couldn't make it out. I'm sorry, he was a good man."

Celise felt the all-too-familiar pang of guilt and sorrow at the mention of Ezri. "He... saved my life," she managed quietly.

"We'll have you join the official ceremony later, but for now, you," he pointed at Syrin, "are to hold the rank of Sergeant." He shifted his arm to aim at Celise, "For yourself, the rank will be Corporal."

He waved them to follow him as he stepped foot deeper into the base. "We'll need to do a proper debrief right away, but it shouldn't be long before we can get you some food and rest."

As the trio stepped further along the makeshift 'street' inside the cavern, Celise couldn't help but feel nervous. It felt as though every passing glance was a mix of mild curiosity and outright suspicion. Not that she could blame them. It hadn't been so long ago that she and Syrin had been the *enemy*.

Two Days Later

The small alcove where hand-to-hand sparring had been seen was rapidly converted into a briefing area. Captain Reeves stood at the front by a table, next to a pair of others in Commonwealth military uniforms Celise couldn't decipher. As the group of milling fighters settled down, Celise and Syrin found a pair of seats on the edge of the third row. A young man and woman to their side offered a warm smile, and a discreet wave as the presentation was about to begin.

Celise hadn't expected just how welcoming the loyalist fighters were going to be. If the stories from the early days of the war were to be believed, defectors were rarely, if ever, taken in. However, the more the fighting progressed, the better it seemed to have gotten. After their initial debriefing, Celise and Syrin had been brought into the makeshift mess hall. Following some short introductions, they were welcomed with open arms. A few of the soldiers even started cheering. Reeves had explained they were cheering the defectors' success in breaking free of the machine.

"Listen up," Captain Reeves began, and the remainder of the chatter came to a quick halt. The evening air was pleasant, but his tone was colder than usual. The faces of the warriors around them reflected a mild curiosity.

"This is the big one." A few faces leaned in, studying the officer. "Tomorrow, we march not as a cell but as a collective. Tomorrow, we will be linking up with **nine** other operations. At dawn, we fight under the banner of a *free* Mars."

His audience watched, transfixed. Celise felt a rising sensation in her chest, a feeling she had not had in a long time. Hope.

"I have with me," Captain Reeves gestured to the two other officers at the front, "some help. These are Agent Stel, and Chief Layroak of the Commonwealth Intelligence Bureau. Chief?" Reeves took a step back, motioning to the short woman on her left.

"Thank you, Captain. This operation has been in planning for many months now, and is the culmination of hard work, and sacrifice, that we have all been waiting for." She paused, sweeping her gaze across the assembly of deadly efficiency.

"As your Captain stated, you will be joining with other loyalist groups to form a large fighting force. Moreover, the Commonwealth has managed to assemble, in secret, a 6,000-strong force of SSG operatives."

A sharp cheer rose from the crowd, and Chief Layroak raised a hand. "Agent Stel and I will be leading this supporting force. Now, your Captain has the specifics on our target." Reeves stepped forward again.

"The target is an MDS convoy travelling through the Abalos Undae dune. We have solid intelligence to suggest that no less than 85% of the Martian government will be within this convoy."

Syrin sucked in her breath. She had heard of "Operation Pole" for a long time but had never been allowed access. Distractedly, she wondered what kind of source the loyalists must have to know about it.

"Sergeants, stick around for further information. Everyone else, get some rest. You'll need it."

Celise rolled over once more to stare out of the small alcove that served as her cot. As rocks went, she didn't think it was so bad.

With a heavy sigh of exasperation, Celise shifted upright, leaning back against the stone. The sub cavern she was in had three other carve-outs within it. Standing up, Celise moved slowly to avoid waking her 'roommates,' and rubbed her temples gently. She had just reached the entrance to their little asylum when she heard it. A cry, soft in nature, young in stature, and unmistakable in familiarity.

Celise spun, all the fog of her attempted slumber vanishing with an eerie rapidity. Her vision swam, tunnelled until she could see only the 'cot' from which the sound had originated. Her feet were moving quickly before she told them to do any such thing. Her mind, too, was in motion—though running in the opposite direction. Celise reached out one arm towards the trembling figure. The motion felt strange, foreign to her senses. As though it was not *her* orders that the arm was following. In a shock, Celise tried desperately to pull back on the rogue limb, to deny its will. Her efforts were in vain, futile to the utmost, as her hand closed on the crying form's shoulder.

The body turned with no motion of its arms or legs. It rotated until its face was finally revealed, staring blankly ahead.

Celise recoiled sharply, yanking herself free of the powerful translucent grip. The face that looked back was one she knew, and recognized, but had not seen in a long time. It was... her.

"Why didn't you save me?" she said. Celise realized, belatedly, that she wasn't sure whose mouth was moving. The reflection's skin was glossy, fading.

"What?" she tried to say, but what rolled out instead seemed a random assortment of noise. The mirror'd self snapped upright in a powerful, sudden gesture. Her eyes locked forward, and tears began to flow.

"Why? Why didn't you save me?" Celise felt a pull on her side, and whirled around. She froze.

Standing in a semicircle around her were... bodies. Their eyes were vacant. Forms perforated with the signatures of gunfire.

Talia's mouth didn't move; it stayed as it was, hung open in an expression of fear, and anguish. Words emanated all the same.

"Why, Celise? Why wasn't it you?" Celise tried to command her voice, to take charge of her form, but failed utterly. The next corpse in line spoke to her.

"Why, Cel? You said we would win; why?" Rai's eyes looked nowhere and everywhere as a stream of blood poured continuously from his gaping wound.

"Why? Why did you condemn me? What had I done?" Lyan's soft cry cut through the pain in Celise's mind. She felt the first trickles of water on her cheeks.

Celise struck out against her muscles with all her might, trying in vain to keep staring forward, but was inevitably twisted to her side once more.

"Why, Mum? Why did I die?" Markil's tiny, innocent voice sounded so far away. She was looking directly at him, but he would not meet her gaze. His reflection merely stared blankly frontward, looking at nothing in particular.

Celise felt the wave rising from within. The pressure built, grew stronger, and grew more fierce. At last, it broke free in a scream of sorrow most pure.

Celise's eyes snapped open, her war drum thumping rapidly in her chest. Syrin stood over her small alcove. Tears flowed freely from her wife's tightly shut eyes, and Celise's hand shot up on instinct to brush them away.

Syrin blinked, her mouth parting briefly, allowing a single sob to escape.

"Hey," Celise spoke softly, her voice a whisper, barely audible in her own mind over the din of fear. Syrin moved her own hands to wipe away at her face.

"I'm alright, it was... it was only a dream." Her words sounded false, but they seemed to calm Syrin, whose tears were flowing more slowly.

"This—" Syrin breathed out between stifled cries. "This wasn't supposed to be you." Celise's brow furrowed, but she remained silent. Syrin rose from the edge of Celise's cot, her hands moving of their own accord to straighten her uniform.

She cleared her throat and turned to face Celise again. "This," she gestured around them, "the fight, I mean. This was supposed to be... mine. *My* burden."

Celise shifted onto her shoulder, wiping at her own latent tears. She reached out to take her wife's hand in her own.

"I know you feel that way, but this was my choice. I'm... here, now. There's no going back." With each word spoken, her strength seemed to be returning to her, and then to Syrin.

A synthesized voice echoed across the rock walls, rolling its way to their ears from speakers somewhere above.

"All personnel, report to your assigned vehicles. We are moving out."

Syrin pushed the last remnants of her visible sorrows away and helped Celise to her feet to do the same.

"Once more?" The hero smiled. "Once more."

9

Dust to Dust

30th of October, 2252
Five Hours Later

"I heard my friend cry, and he sank to his knees
Coughing blood as he screamed for his mother
And I fell by his side, and that's how we died
Clinging like kids to each other"

The smoke was easy. Celise and Syrin had long since gotten used to the inability to see, the clogging of the lungs, and the overpowering of the scent. What Celise had yet to get used to, or at least what she had yet to accept, was the volume.

"Say again! Come in!" she screamed into the receiver as more rounds whipped through the air above. The whine of engines and the cacophonous explosions of missiles drowned out all communication. Angry, she slammed the device down, and moved swiftly to the trench wall.

Syrin stood on a parapet, firing continuously, then ducking down to relay orders and issue commands to the team. The convoy hit had started off well. The ambush was well-timed, and the SSG force had unleashed volley after volley, destroying the core of security.

Now, they had been sitting in a trench for hours. The convoy had constricted, coiling into a protective circle around itself. With everyone so close together, the Commonwealth forces couldn't risk airstrikes, lest the capture targets be killed.

So, they had been reduced to their small arms and short-range rockets. Celise flinched as another fighter toppled to the ground from the wall in front of her. Then she sucked in her breath and took his place.

Celise spotted the shooter who had dispatched her comrade with ease, the glint of his rifle's scope made him a magnet for her fire. She felt a hand on her arm, and turned to one side, ducking down below the firing line. A young soldier was tugging on her sleeve, pointing his free arm wildly to their left side.

With a start, she saw it. A small form darted from one rock to another on the raised area just outside the trench. Celise knew her voice wouldn't reach the others in time, but she had something much louder than a shout.

Celise swung her rifle quickly to bear on the forms that had begun to emerge en masse. Her finger tightened on the trigger, and the effect worked... on her immediate surroundings. Those soldiers, close enough to care about the minor change in the direction of gunfire, snapped around. They saw quickly what she had fired at, and too levelled their weapons.

Those other soldiers, those fighters further away, didn't have time to react. The enemy's surprise flanking attack worked overwhelmingly on them, and bodies began crumpling. Between bursts, Celise managed a glance to her right, and breathed a sigh of relief. Syrin had noticed the attack, and was returning fire from cover.

Celise sprinted to the opposite side of the trench wall, and started moving quickly, methodically, down the line. A soldier was stood in front of her as she rounded a bend. She suddenly realized he was sporting an MDS uniform.

The man's gun snapped up in front of him, his finger closing on the trigger. With a jolt, he staggered to his side, and collapsed. Syrin hurried to Celise's side, placing a steadying hand on her shoulder.

"We've still got a war to win." Her words were antagonistic to the softness of her tone, and Celise nodded the affirmative.

Side by side, the pair continued moving down the trench line. Stopping briefly whenever there was a foe to dispatch or a friend to aid. At last, they came to the end of the line, from where they could exit the trench and come up behind the ambushers.

Syrin scanned out the opening with her eyes, then raised one hand and gestured for Celise to follow.

"Stay close," she muttered under her breath. Then, she took a cautionary first step outside the relative safety of the trench. Celise followed behind, her own weapon in the ready position, her eyes blinking rapidly in an attempt to keep out the dust. They walked carefully, quietly, until finally coming up behind the very rocks that had been used against them.

Syrin took a half-step forward before seeing that Celise wasn't moving.

"Cel!" she whispered, "We need to go!" Celise stared down at one of the bodies littering the ground. Her expression was buried beneath a mask of stoicism.

Darek Shay's glossy eyes stared up at her. A small, neat hole ruined the perfect symmetry of his uniform. A hand touched her back gently.

"Celise. We can't stay here." Her wife's voice shook her from her thoughts. Wordlessly, Celise re-gripped her rifle, and returned to Syrin's side. Syrin counted down from three on her fingers, and the pair sprang out from behind the low cover.

What remained of the MDS force was hunkered down in a single pit, suppressed by oncoming fire from other angles of the trench. Syrin and Celise raised their weapons, and fired. The brief exchange was over in a matter of seconds, and the pair dropped back down into the trench to assess their wounded.

Before they could get a chance at respite, a private ran up to them, carrying a long-range comms device.

"Sergeant Valen, sir!" She was out of breath, and Syrin held up a hand to give her pause.

After a few deep inhales, the messenger could speak again. "Sergeant, new orders from Captain Reeves. We are to join the trench in sector four at once." Celise whistled, and the faces of soldiers around them mirrored her own anxiety.

Syrin simply nodded. "We have our orders, then," she addressed the rest of her team. "Everyone, treat the wounded as best you can. Those that can run, rendezvous on the East wall. Those who can't will have to stay here."

There were a few quiet murmurs, but the soldiers disbanded quickly, moving to assume their duties.

The line of soldiers along the trench wall would have been impressive if not for their utterly ragged appearance. The line trembled and quaked with every turbulent blast of missile landing ever closer. Celise squeezed Syrin's hand tightly and stared into her eyes.

"We'll be okay," Celise whispered. It was more a plea than a statement. Syrin forced a smile and nodded with vigour.

"I love you," she whispered back. Celise retrieved her rifle from her shoulder and gripped it firmly across her chest. Syrin's eyes swept the line one last time, then she unclipped the ringer from her belt, and clicked it twice.

The shrill alarm sounded in the trench, giving her team their orders. As one, a mass of force emerged from the trench, climbing rapidly up the ladders and ducking into a full sprint. The distance to the other trench, where their orders had directed them to go, was not so far.

Celise kept her eyes locked straight ahead as she ran. The weight of the gun in her hands felt exponentially heavier than usual, and for a moment, she contemplated whether she should simply drop it.

Celise did not dwell on the thought for long, for the next thing she knew, she was tumbling face-first towards the ground. A scorching, red-hot paint lanced across her body, and a scream clambered and rocketed from her throat.

The dust climbed upon her, claiming her as she twisted and writhed within it. A gloved hand touched her cheek, and through her fading cone of vision, she saw Syrin's face of terror watching her. Celise saw the tears first, then she saw the red. The beautiful, elegant, bright-red horror spilling out of her wife's chest in a sudden violence.

Syrin's face contorted in the pain, then relaxed as her eyes drifted away from purpose. Celise tried desperately to cry out, scream louder, and refuse this reality. She did not succeed.

With a final relinquishing of control, Syrin succumbed to the effort, and collapsed upon her. At last, the small voice of resistance within Celise caved in on itself, and her eyes fluttered shut.

Epilogue
Between the Crosses

14th of March, 2253
Five Months Later

"Do you feel like a hero yet?"

Maks Norvu looked out the window of the landing short-range transport. The trip from Earth to the Martian Orbital Platform had been quite comfortable, and he enjoyed having time to catch up on the films.

He searched the signs hanging from the station's roof for the correct line and walked over.

"Purpose?" the man standing behind a small divider asked. His form was sleeved in the uniform of the Commonwealth's **Orbital Defence Corps**. Maks offered a polite smile.

"Records collection," he replied, and the ODC officer keyed in a code on his private panel. "Agency?" Maks passed the small signet from his collar through the depositing chamber.

"Arbiter's Office for the Historical Preservation of the Martian Rebellion." The title was a bit of a mouthful, but the officer simply nodded and keyed another set of instructions.

"You should know, it's now the Civil War. Arbiters just affirmed the new wording a few minutes ago; you were probably still on board." The officer passed the signet back to Maks, who reattached it to his suit.

"Thanks for the notice," the man's final keyed-in instruction opened the gate, and he waved Maks through. "Safe travels."

Norvu stepped off the transport a few minutes after it touched down in the Martian capital. Despite the significant amount of resources committed to reconstruction, it was slow-going, and the capital was still largely in ruins. The Commonwealth had focused primarily on infrastructure first, and buildings second. This, Maks reasoned, was why the landing pad was a skeletal foundation.

He quickly checked the directions screen but couldn't see his destination. He frowned slightly and approached the arrival's desk.

"Welcome to Mars!" The cheeriness of the deck officer startled him slightly, but Maks recovered quickly.

"Thank you, I'm searching for passage to Abalos Undae, but I don't see it on the list?" The officer, whose uniform Maks didn't recognize, lost the smile quickly.

"Oh, I'm sorry, sir, but that region of the planet is still off-limits."

Norvu shook his head a little, offering a placating smile. "I'm sure for most, yes. I've been sent here by the Arbiters, however. I'm a historian, you see?" He passed her the signet, and she glanced it over. After a few brief moments, she seemed to decide to believe him.

"Sorry, I've never worked this shift before. The train in bay 17 is heading for Abalos Colles. You should be able to find a way from there."

Maks smiled and thanked the deck officer. Then, he retrieved his case, and made his way toward the rail bays.

***

The train ride was a long one, and by the time Maks woke up (and realized he had fallen asleep), he was sure that at least a day had gone by. He checked the train compartment's screen quickly and confirmed his suspicions. It was the 15th, alright.

Norvu looked out the window of the car. He thought he could see a small village on the horizon, but he couldn't be sure at that distance.

The train came to a gentle stop, and Maks frowned in confusion until he turned to look out the other side's window. He had arrived at the central station for the North. From here, he would have to go manual.

Stepping off the car, Maks breathed in deeply. There were few places, easily accessible, that is, in the solar system, that still felt like this. They felt very far away, very peaceful. He liked that feeling. Maks looked around, and, spotting his target, made his way to a vehicle rental stand. From the vendor, he traded some Commonwealth Valoro for a transport, then set off along the only road that went North.

Maks nearly fell on his face as he tripped over another body. He turned and gazed at it curiously. This one was half buried under a layer of dust so thick he had almost missed it.

Sighing, he set down his case and retrieved a blower. He powered up the device and fired gusts of gentle winds over the form until it became recognizable. *Oh*, Maks corrected himself. *Forms.* There were two here; one lay across the other.

Norvu crouched down, reaching a gloved hand toward the topmost corpse. He searched up its arm near the shoulder, hoping for an easily identifiable patch. Finding none, he gently pulled on the body, turning it to see the other arm. There, he could make out the remnants of a fading Commonwealth flag on the shoulder.

Maks twisted the form all the way around, taking it off the second so that they lay side by side. He wrinkled his nose at the protruding hole in the first soldier's chest; it was terribly off-centre.

Reaching down, he brushed a small layer of dust off the lapel, to find a waiting signet. Maks stood and retrieved the device from his case. He navigated through menus and submenus, eventually arriving at the Commonwealth Ground Forces, subsection Sergeants. His gloved finger depressed the small button labelled **+1**.

He pocketed the device and turned his work to the second body. This one's Commonwealth flag was much more visible. It had been hidden underneath the other soldier's hand, protected from the dust. Maks reached down to examine the signet and smiled a little. *Easy.* He navigated one section up on his device, then one across, to find CGF subsection Corporals.

He pressed **+1**.

THE END

Thank you for reading.

If you are interested in more of my work,
visit ashoward.ca

~ ASH

9 781738 280124